If only Rusty could talk and tell their story. Talk? David leaped to his feet and flung his arms about the startled bird.

"Rusty!" he shouted gleefully. "You can do it! You can save me! A message to the outside world. Airmail even. Why, you may go down in history as the largest carrier pigeon of all time!"

As though he somehow understood, Rusty, caught up in the boy's excitement, wormed from his embrace, picked up a stick, and began to dance.

David cut a metal sheet from a tin can, then poring over his maps, punched tiny holes in the tin with the point of his knife to show the location of the wrecked plane, the numbers on the wings, his approximate route of travel, the big river flowing north, the bald hill, the cabin, and the date as he guessed it. He included, too, his stepfather's name and address and the letters SOS.

He held the tin up against the sky for easier reading and, satisfied it was legible, folded the tin into a leg band. Shaking in his excitement, he caught the crane in his arms, bent the strip snugly around one of Rusty's long legs, and twisted the ends together.

"You've got to make it, Rusty. You're my last chance."

ABOUT THE AUTHOR

Dayton O. Hyde has used his talents as a writer to advance the cause of conservation, especially the preservation of endangered species of waterfowl. He is a director of the International Wild Waterfowl Association and of the Oregon Wildlife Federation. He lives on a ranch in Oregon.

Strange Companion

A Story of Survival

---

by DAYTON O. HYDE

Illustrations by Jim Santiago

Winner of the Dutton Animal Book Award

A FAWCETT CREST BOOK

Fawcett Publications, Inc., Greenwich, Connecticut

STRANGE COMPANION

THIS BOOK CONTAINS THE COMPLETE TEXT OF
THE ORIGINAL HARDCOVER EDITION.

A Fawcett Crest Book reprinted by arrangement with
E.P. Dutton & Company, Inc.

Copyright © 1975 by Dayton O. Hyde

ALL RIGHTS RESERVED

ISBN: 0-449-23298-0

Selection of The Good Reading Club
Selection of Better Homes and Gardens Family Book
Service

Printed in the United States of America

10 9 8 7 6 5 4 3 2 1

To Malcolm Reiss

One

DAVID heard his stepfather shouting to him as he fled down the hill from the barn. The words pelted him as he plunged through the branches of an aspen thicket, leaped over a brook of melting snow, and squeezed through a windbreak of spruce.

"David! David! You come back here now or I'll whale you good!" The angry summons began to fade out just as he'd heard it fade out so often in his dreams, for in his dreams he'd run away many times.

Many a night he'd sought out his cot up under the eaves of the old farmhouse, and as the cottonwood trees, churned by the restless winds of the Canadian prairies, clawed against the unpainted boards, he'd vowed that the next time the old man got mad at him, he'd leave home for good, even if he was just thirteen and a half, and go off somewhere, maybe south to the United States.

Often as he lay listening to planes from the Edmonton airport droning directly overhead on their way to cities he'd only read about, he thought about hitching a ride on one. Maybe to Calgary, where every year they held the big rodeo and the chuck wagon races and where he could earn food taking care of horses and tack. Or maybe to Vancouver, on the west coast, where he could hire out to the captain of a fishing boat.

Things were always worse after Kise had been to the cemetery. He'd put on his black store-bought pants, the seat shiny from many a Sunday rub on a church pew, button a white collar awkwardly about his Adam's apple, gather some wildflowers from the meadow or, in winter, weave a garland of spruce tips, then climb into his battered pickup truck for the trip to David's mother's grave. He always went alone, as though he'd never found a way to share his grief with her boy. And when he got back it always seemed that he was madder than ever at life for taking her away.

Times like that, hard as he tried, David couldn't seem to do anything to please. Last week, his head full of spring and bird song, he had forgotten to close the garden gate, and the spavined old draft team, which Kise preferred to expensive tractors, came nosing in to trample the rhubarb. Moments ago, while milking Parsnip, the big speckled Holstein cow, that ornery biddy had snorted at a rooster stealing grain out of her feed box and kicked the new milk bucket right through the window of the barn.

Kise had heard the commotion from the house and come on the run. Hearing a door slam, David had vaulted into the haymow, then crossed the manger into the horse stalls. "Easy, boys," he had pleaded as he squeezed between the huge work horses, lowered himself through the manure window, and escaped into the adjoining woods.

Right now Kise would be turning loose the hounds, and the dogs would follow fast, sniffing the ground, zigzagging, yelping as they picked up David's scent, trailing him without comprehending that they were betraying someone they loved.

But David had thought this out too, and as he paused for a moment to listen, he heard first the excited music of old Speck and then of Melinda as they joined in a duet on his trail. As he had planned so many times before, he plunged into the thickets of willow that grew thick along the creek bank.

A huge lop-eared snowshoe rabbit, still wearing his white winter coat, thumped a warning to his mates, then charged out from his usual hiding place beneath a windfall, and scampered away.

The boy had used this ruse before, knowing full well the hounds would switch to the rabbit's trail. Soon the old man would be crashing through the tangles, trying to keep up with the hounds as the snowshoe made his typical big circle and returned to his log, while David himself would be safely across the stream and away.

But before he left the shelter of the thickets, he paused beneath an old cottonwood tree, and standing on tiptoe, reached one arm into a deserted owl's nest in the hollow trunk and pulled out a battered pipe tobacco can, which served as his treasure chest. Inside was a rumpled handful of money his mom had given him. He counted it nervously, as though fearing that the scant inheritance he had been hoarding for just such an emergency would somehow be less than he remembered. Thirty-nine—no, forty dollars. It was all there. He tucked the money deep in an inner pocket.

Balancing on a slippery log, he crossed the river. He heard the fresh clamor of the hounds as they scented the rabbit and raced away. Then Kise's voice, anger muffled by distance. For a long moment he stood watching, then, satisfied he had thrown Kise off his trail, he moved on.

The gravel road winding along the bluffs seemed deserted as he strode toward the distant city. From a roadside fence post a flicker drummed insults to a rival, and the first swallows worked the pastures restlessly for early insects, as though worried that they had wandered north too soon. At that moment David would have given anything to be one of them, skimming wild and free over the awakening land.

In the distance he saw a farmer plowing the blackened wheat stubble with a bright orange tractor. David waved and the man waved back. Across the river he could see a yellow school bus picking up children for school, and he wondered what Clanahan, the bus driver, would think when he slowed down at Kise's farm and he, David, failed to show.

He was almost out of the country and in the suburbs of the city, where he would be safe from detection, when suddenly around the bend rumbled a battered milk delivery truck, driven by Kise's friend and cribbage partner, Elmore Claridge.

"Whoah!" shouted Mr. Claridge. Having only recently traded in his ancient delivery horses for the truck, he had yet to master its workings and skidded to a stop with a clash of gears. "Ho, David. Wouldn't be off to play hooky again, would you, lad?" The old man had stringy gray hair, faded blue eyes that were narrowed with suspicion of all youth. He had often sermonized Kise on how to bring up David, though he'd never raised a child of his own.

"It's Saturday, Mr. Claridge," David replied.

"Saturday? Merciful heavens, so 'tis. So 'tis! See you tomorrow, David, in church." With a chattering squeal the truck leaped into gear and was soon gone.

It was really Friday. David felt guilty that he had confused the old man, for now the day was fixed hard and fast in his head. He'd deliver milk to his Saturday customers, mostly weekend folks, while the Friday route went without.

David strode on, across fields and down suburban streets. A couple of hours passed and his jacket, which had kept off the chill of early morning, now seemed unpleasantly warm. David removed it and bundled it under his arm. Now and again he saw planes in the distance descending and ascending to and from the city airport. If he were on a plane, in moments he would be over new lands. Guided by the planes, he moved with quickened pace toward the airport.

As he neared his destination, a huge jet airliner leaped into the air, and passed directly over David's head. He covered his ears against the racket; the planes he had seen at a distance had made a pleasant drone, nothing like this.

His heart pounded as he approached the airport terminal and slipped through the doors. For a few minutes he stood in back of the eddying crowd, watching warily for friends of Kise, teachers, neighbors, or anyone who might recognize him and send him home. When no one seemed to notice him, he joined an island of travelers drifting down a corridor. Had any of them given him a second glance, they would have seen a thin, not-too-clean farm boy, with dark intelligent eyes, wearing homemade clothes that had been patched and repatched with a bachelor's square, no-nonsense stitches. A fistfull of goosegrease could not have tamed his thick unruly hair.

With one of his precious dollars he bought some candy bars and a comic book, deliberating over his selections as though they were his last decisions on earth.

As he entered a room crowded with passengers awaiting flights, he saw, too late, that he had been noticed by a policeman, who broke off a conversation to advance toward him as though to question him. David's heart fluttered, but he walked briskly along.

"Wait up, young un," the policeman called.

David's step slowed a bit, then, mercifully, an elderly woman rose from her seat and grasped the officer by the elbow. Within moments David was at the ticket counter, waiting in line for his turn. He hoped that the policeman would have forgotten him.

"One way to Calgary," David said, trying to act as though flying were an everyday thing for him. He laid down a fistful of moist bills on the counter.

The agent swept them away. "Calgary, eh?" He glanced down at the boy. "How old are you, son?"

"I—uh—" In a blind panic David turned and ran, leaving the startled ticket agent with the sum of his inheritance.

Rushing into the adjoining waiting room, he glanced back and saw the man at the counter lift a telephone. Moments later the policeman entered the waiting room and passed rapidly back and forth, scanning faces hidden behind newspapers.

David rushed down the long corridor. Blocked suddenly by a locked door at the end of the hall, he darted through an entrance marked No Admittance. Airport Personnel Only and found himself in an airplane hangar. The odor of spilled gasoline was almost overpowering.

He had no time to look about. Hearing the click and scuff of boot heels on his trail, he leaped behind a stack of oxygen tanks. From the doorway the round face of the policeman loomed like a pale moon as he surveyed the scene.

"Maybe I ought to give myself up and let them send me back to the farm," David thought, feeling more than a little scared.

But he was still angry with his stepfather. He'd show Kise he could take care of himself.

He waited in silence, nearly choking from fumes in his musty corner. His throat tickled, and one leg tingled like crazy where it had gone to sleep. Suddenly the policeman turned and moved off up the hall. David listened with relief as the footsteps became fainter, then died away entirely.

From the shelter of a pile of oil drums, he watched as two mechanics serviced a large twin-engined Grumman amphibian. Airplanes were special to David, and he remembered seeing this one fly over the farm the day before. It had been a thrill, since on the prairies there wasn't much need for a plane that could land on both land and water.

On the side of the plane was an emblem of a flying goose and a leaping fish, with the words "U.S. Department of the Interior, Fish and Wildlife Service." Rather than Calgary he'd try the States, maybe even get a job picking oranges, where he could get all the fruit he wanted to eat as part of his pay.

The workmen took their lunch pails and Thermos bottles and moved off to eat in the spring sunshine. David rose quickly and moved to the plane, crawled up on the wing, pulled open the door, and crept inside. Forward, in the cockpit, he caught a glimpse of rows of instruments. Dials, knobs, levers, each with some mysterious function. Moving back toward the tail section, he crawled into the dark cargo hold and made a nest in a pile of canvas.

As he lay waiting for whatever the future would bring, suddenly he felt proud of what he had accomplished. But then, close on the heels of his pride, came a nagging doubt that he deserved any credit at all. Maybe the aircraft had been waiting there in the hangar for him to come along.

He lay back in his hideaway. Soon the plane would take off, leaving Edmonton and all the world he had ever known far behind.

Two

ONE morning in early April, nearly two thousand miles south of David and Edmonton, an Audubon Society biologist sat in his blind observing three rare whooping cranes as they probed for blue crabs in a coastal marsh. Because of the society's great concern for the survival of this species, they had given top priority to a study of the giant white birds on their last-remaining wintering grounds, those tidal flats and low brushy hills along the Texas Gulf that constitute the Aransas National Wildlife Refuge.

Since dawn it had been a routine watch, but now the biologist noted a restlessness in the birds. They tossed bits of seaweed or driftwood into the air with their long, saberlike beaks, and whirled into the flapping, leaping dance for which they are famous. Then, for a time, the two white adults, together with their still-rusty offspring of the previous year, preened silently before resuming their nervous antics. "Kerloo! Kerloo!" they called and the marshes echoed with their trumpeting.

The biologist looked at his wrist watch, then made an entry in his field notebook. Picking up the receiver from his small portable telephone, he flipped a switch, blew into the mouthpiece to check its operation, then cranked the generator handle.

"Refuge Headquarters." The woman's voice was almost blown away by ocean winds sweeping in over the salt-grass dunes.

"Carol? This is Bill Sterling. Can you hear me? Look, I'm in a blind on the southwest shore of Mustang Lake. Get hold of your boss immediately—at home and in the shower if necessary—and tell him crane family number eight might be getting ready to head north. They're dancing, calling—the whole bit. I know he'll want to alert personnel along the migration route. And if he wants in-flight observations as the birds leave the refuge, he'd better radio his pilot to stand by the aircraft. I'll keep in touch, of course, and call you the moment the birds are airborne."

Hanging up, the biologist raised his binoculars for a quick survey, first of the birds, then of the surrounding refuge. Across the lake he could see a group of tourists on the public observation tower, crowded around the big telescope awaiting turns to watch the behavior of the cranes. It pleased him that the group seemed interested. All too often, he suspected, visitors to the tower were distracted by wild turkeys, deer, and peccaries grubbing for acorns in the brush below and thus missed the antics of the whoopers, one of North America's largest, rarest, and most spectacular birds.

Far down the waterway he could see the excursion boat "Birdwatcher" headed his way with its daily load of sightseers. Another time he wouldn't have minded, but now he cursed under his breath, fearful that the approaching boat might cause the birds to fly to another feeding area beyond his field of view.

He pictured his friend Captain Bowen at the helm, gray at the temples, doing his usual fervent job over the intercom of lecturing his passengers about nature and endangered species in general and the whooping crane in particular.

By now Bowen would have spotted the cranes feeding in the shallows up ahead and would be alerting his passengers to ready their cameras as he slowed his pounding engines and coasted in for a closer look.

"Go on past, Cap," he pleaded, but the captain had no way of hearing, no way of knowing of his blind. Already he could see a huddle of excited passengers crowding the rail, barrage of cameras ready. He glanced once more at the cranes. The female and the young bird still fed quietly in the shallows, but the great male now stood upright watching the approaching boat.

DAYTON O. HYDE

Captain Bowen whistled under his breath as he saw the three cranes feeding along the shore. It had already been a fabulous trip. There were days when the birds were off feeding or loafing elsewhere, and try as he might, he couldn't show his passengers a single crane. There were always persons who, having traveled across half a continent to see the cranes, left the boat muttering that the ride along the edge of the refuge was a waste of time and money.

But today he had been able to show them a large group of the birds feeding and dancing in a grain field planted especially for the cranes by refuge personnel. If the total population this side of extinction was forty-three, it meant that his customers had observed more than half the existing birds. Those cranes had been standing at a good distance from the canal; now the three cranes up ahead would provide the people on the boat with a closer look.

The trio of cranes seemed almost to ignore the boat as Bowen slackened speed, steadied the prow against a handy sandbar, and shut off the engines entirely so that the tourists could hold their cameras steady.

Slowly, necks outstretched suspiciously, the cranes moved out of the shallows and stalked toward shore, measuring the ground with each stately step. A reverent hush crept over the spectators, broken only by the click and whir of cameras.

Suddenly, already nervous and excited from the irrepressible forces of migration welling within, the cranes moved away. It was as though they felt they had suffered indignities enough from such scrutiny. With great long strides the birds ran a short distance into the wind, spread their great black-tipped wings, and lofted into the air, leaving boat, blind, and observation tower behind. The sound of their trumpeting fell as a farewell over the refuge. Higher and higher they circled and soon disappeared among the lowering clouds.

The pilot waiting beside his small plane had already warmed his engines when the signal came from refuge headquarters that the cranes had left the refuge. Moments later he too was airborne, circling his craft up through the thick gray cotton of scudding cumulus. As he glimpsed the blue sky overhead, he contacted the refuge, knowing the whole staff would be clustered in the super's office awaiting his report.

"Piper 139 to Headquarters. Boss Man, do you read me?"

"Headquarters to Piper 139. This is Boss Man, as you put it. Lots of static this morning but we read you. What's going on up there? Over."

"Piper 139 to Headquarters. Three cranes circling at about ten thousand feet, two miles west. Might be sandhill cranes instead of whoopers. Hey! I can see the sun flashing on white feathers. Definitely whoopers! Gaining altitude fast. Over."

"Headquarters to Piper 139. Don't get too close. The point is to observe normal and not harassed behavior. If you can, establish at what altitude they finally line out and begin their journey. And give us some idea of wind directions and velocities at that elevation. If a ground wind from the south induces them to migrate, I'd like to know if they find a similar air current up high. Do your best, but don't risk your neck. Over."

"Piper 139 to Headquarters. I've done about all I can up here. The birds are at fifteen thousand and still rising. If I go any higher I'll need astronaut's gear."

"Headquarters to Piper 139. Again, don't take chances. Watch them as long as possible and do try to estimate the elevation. If we have that, the military or the commercial airlines may be able to give us air currents and velocities. Once you've lost them better head downstairs. OK? Over."

"Piper 139 to Headquarters. I read you. Call them at Charley's and tell them to warm up a pot of coffee. Over and out."

For a few minutes after the radio conversation had ceased, the supervisor of the Aransas Refuge sat at his desk reflecting. His face was gray with fatigue. At no other refuge in the world was the pressure greater than at Aransas when the whooping cranes were in residence. Much as he loved the big birds, it was with the greatest relief that he watched them leave the refuge for their far-off nesting grounds.

As far as he could determine, two precious whoopers had been lost during the winter. One had flown into a power transmission line near the refuge, and the other may have been shot by vandals, although reports of a dead whooping crane across the Mexican border had not been confirmed in spite of extensive searches. The deaths had not been his fault, but still, down deep, he took the blame.

The first crane family had now left the refuge; in the days to come the rest would leave in small groups and large until all were gone. Then the pressure would be off until the following autumn, when they would come straggling in again with such young as they had been able to produce.

Now with migration under way it was time to double-check protective measures along the whooping crane flyway, where most losses occurred. He called in his assistant, and within minutes the machinery set up months before was in motion. In every town and hamlet along the route, lectures, articles in local newspapers, interviews on radio and television, all by competent personnel, warned hunters not to shoot the big white birds. Additional wardens patrolled the back roads, and a vast network of thousands of local bird watchers and sportsmen kept up a twenty-four-hour-a-day crane watch and reported their sightings to authorities.

The telephone rang; it was the Audubon Society biologist again. Two more whooping crane families and five unmated birds had taken to the air and disappeared into the cloud cover. As he placed the phone back in its cradle he sighed. He had done everything within his power. The rest was up to the cranes.

High above Aransas the pilot shivered in the thin upper air and zipped his heavy flight jacket up to his chin. However good a cup of hot coffee would taste to him, some streak of stubbornness within made him continue on. Above him he could see the cranes circling in the bright sunlight of the upper air. Their plumage shone as dazzling white as new snow on a mountain top and contrasted sharply with the ebony black of the five heavy pinion feathers, which tipped each wing. Circling effortlessly, they drifted slowly upwards as though searching out the proper air current to carry them over Saint Charles Bay toward their northern nesting grounds, nearly three thousand miles away. Soon the birds seemed to find a current to their liking, but it was far above the range at which the pilot could fly without special equipment. He watched them in frustration as they left their wintering grounds behind and began their awesome journey. Only when they were mere specks far above and beyond him did he turn back, nosing his plane down through the gray coastal cloud bank toward the land below.

As the sun climbed to its zenith, then waned and set behind the mountains to the west, the trio of whooping cranes beat steadily on, circling at times to lift over ramparts of thunderheads and sailing high over twinkling lights of cities, over Texas plains nodding with bluebonnets, and over the skeletal oil derricks of Oklahoma. On the second day they looked down upon emerald checkerboards of Kansas wheat and rolling, cattle-dotted Nebraska prairies until at last, on the third day, they descended to rest on an isolated sandbar in the River Platte.

For a few days the trio rested along the Platte, sunning themselves, preening, bathing, drinking, and making regular forays into neighboring agricultural areas for food. Once another whooping crane family joined them for the night as they roosted in a shallow backwater of the river, but they did not mingle and in the morning the newcomers flew off upstream and did not return.

Once more the restless urges of migration seized the cranes, and rain pelting their feathers, they flew off without so much as a backward glance at the quiet reaches of river below. Spiraling up toward the upper limits of the atmosphere, the crane family passed northward over South Dakota and North Dakota, cut across a corner of Montana, and cruised across the international border into Saskatchewan, where at last, craving food and rest, they settled down upon a vast acreage of newly sprouted grain.

They fed and preened, resting calmly, as though as they approached the north some of the hurry had gone out of them. More probably, however, they sensed the approach of the sudden spring storm that was roaring down out of the north, covering the greening fields with a foot of snow.

For all migrating birds it was a time of peril. Flung helter-skelter by tempestuous gales gathering force across the treeless prairies, even the hardy pipits and horned larks searched in vain for seeds, and the first swallows to invade the area clustered under barn eaves for shelter, but lacking sufficient insect food for body heat, they perished during the chill of darkness, and by morning, lay lifeless on the straw heaps outside the stable windows. Many a summer meadow would now be silent because of their absence.

The whooping cranes probed deep in the snow for grain but found none while the violent, gusty blasts of wind ruffled their wing plumes and nearly swept them off their feet. Wings tight to their sides, they folded their long legs and hugged the earth, heads tucked under feathers. Only when the storm had blown itself out and the wet snow had vanished before the gentle persistence of a chinook wind were they able to continue their journey northward, crossing the Athabaska and Slave rivers and going on through northern Alberta into the Northwest Territories.

But spring was late in coming, and when the cranes arrived, their nesting marshes were still icebound. Until the ponds were free to ripple with the winds, the cranes haunted the edges of streams, where patches of open water supplied them with the nymphs and larvae of insects awaiting the dancing time of summer.

However unseasonable the weather, inside the body of the big male crane the hormones were working. The youngster, who had hitherto known only tender care from his parents, looked up one morning from his feeding at the side of his mother to see his father advancing upon him, neck extended, beak like a drawn sword, and yellow eyes sparkling with sudden hatred. For a time, when the young bird ran a few yards away from his mother, the male seemed satisfied. But soon the old patriarch became less and less tolerant and charged the young bird whenever he approached. He had only to land nearby and the father would fly straight toward the poor confused crane and send him flying. Soon the youngster failed to return and probably wandered the northland in solitude for a time until he chanced upon others of his kind.

The male was as tender in his relationship with the female as he was savage in his behavior toward his offspring. The pair fed shoulder to shoulder, heads almost touching as they probed the awakening earth. Now and again the male bugled a ringing, territorial challenge, but since the young bird had vanished and his nearest rival was perhaps a hundred miles away, there was no answer.

May came, and as the mating season approached, it should have been a time of physical well-being, but though the bare red skin atop the male's head grew more scarlet with each passing day, the female's crown remained dull. Her droppings were thin and watery. She spent long hours standing in shallow pools in seeming dejection. Only when the pair drifted at last to their old nesting territory did the female take an interest in the scene around her.

Together they circled the marsh that had been their home for perhaps twenty seasons. On an island of grass just emerging from the water was a faint outline of last year's nest, and in unison they called down as though greeting the spirits of chicks of years past, lost to storms and predators. Their voices echoed from the surrounding forests of dwarf birch, willow, black spruce, and tamarack.

In another year they would have spent much time in the air, flying over their territory, giddy with the sheer joy of being airborne. But this year the male flew mostly alone. Now and again after a flight, the female would sneeze, shake her head, and gasp for breath. Her heavy bill would gape open for a time as though she was having difficulty breathing.

In late May, however, she showed some sign of improvement. Snails were plentiful and the sun beat warm and long upon the earth. All around them life, from the lowliest lichen to the white-crowned sparrows and Tennessee warblers singing so endlessly, seemed determined to use each precious day to reproduce its kind.

One day, as though caught by spring's magic, she began to show some interest in her old nest. She dragged up a few stalks of marsh grass by the roots and began to rebuild the floating platform she had used the previous year. But soon she lost interest and wandered off out of the sunlight to where the shadows of the spruces played over the dark beer-bottle-brown water. Then the next day she was back, determined to build again, and within hours had pulled up the surrounding grasses to form her island.

On this sanctuary she laid her first big egg; it was brown, lavender, and green, as though stained by all the colors of the marshes. As soon as the first was laid, she began her patient incubation as if she was so eager to rest at last that she was unable to await the arrival of the second and final egg of the clutch some three days later.

Now and then she would stand above the eggs and turn them gently with her saberlike beak, clucking softly as though communicating with the developing embryos in the shell. Then she would slip off across the marsh to feed.

When she had gone far enough from the nest so as not to attract such egg-stealing predators as ravens, she would call in her mate from adjoining marshes, and while she fed along the shores, he would visit with her for a time. Then, feeding as he went, he would wade slowly out to the nest, stand for a moment turning the eggs with his bill, glance about for danger, and folding his long black legs neatly beneath him, settle to take his turn with family duties.

Whenever wood buffaloes, moose, or bears wandered past her marsh, she would stick her head straight out before her and crouch motionless, keeping a low profile as though she were only a floating water-bleached stump, until all danger had passed. Let the trespasser but wade the pond, however, and her sudden, nervous bugling summoned the male in from afar. Together they feigned injuries and led the intruder away or grew hostile and drove him off.

For three long weeks the incubation dragged on. The snowy white plumes of the hen grew stained with marsh ooze and needed preening; her bare forehead, once almost crimson, turned to pale rose, then ebbed to an unsightly gray, but still she clung to her duties. Hour after hour during the long heat of the subarctic day she dozed, head buried under her wing, waking only to drink thirstily from the pond and then settle back into her stupor. Once as she sneezed and gaped, a drop of crimson blood splattered her white breast.

If there were days when she managed to feed for a few hours about the marsh on snails and other pond life, there were other days when she left her nest not at all. As though sensing that the companionship of nearly a quarter of a century might soon be ending, the male spent more and more of his time moping in the shadows, his voice filled with desolation.

There was no thunder out of heaven when the old crane died. Rather the pond was mirror calm with the cool hush of morning when her head trailed once or twice into the still waters, her wings flopped spasmodically as though in some last vain instinctive battle to protect her eggs, and then all was still. Only the swallows dared the stillness of the pond, chittering at their reflections as they swooped on graceful wings or, in full flight, caught some tiny midge another bird might have ignored.

In her last moments one egg was somehow broken, but in the other the embryo continued to live, though, as her body cooled, its life processes began, hour by hour, to slow.

Once, twice, the male called to her on the nest, then waded out to stand beside her. His low, throaty endearments went unheard.

Three

DAVID had read his comic book twice through by the dim light of a small window and was trying to catnap away his fears when, suddenly, the plane swayed as the pilot stepped onto the wing, pushed his heavy canvas duffel through the door, and stooped low to enter. For agonizing moments David held his breath as the man peered into the hold, squinting his eyes from the swift change from sunlight to gloom. He swung the bag forward, pinning David's legs, but the boy did not cry out.

He saw the man framed clearly, in the doorway—stout with middle age, his face as red as a turkey gobbler's wattle from exertion, and his ears projecting from his jaunty pilot's cap like perches for a parrot. His worn leather belt, held by a pewter buckle, cut beneath his belly, accentuating its prominence rather than holding it in. His plaid shirt pocket carried three cigars, a fistful of ballpoint pens, and a worn pack of playing cards.

From outside the plane came sounds of a flurry of activity, and the plane jerked forward with a lurch as a tow car pulled it out of the hangar onto the concrete apron. David heard the pilot's window slide open and then voices. He was conversing with someone on the ground.

"A runaway kid on my plane? You kidding? Why, on this run the government has trouble hiring observers to ride with me."

The pilot turned in his seat and shouted aft. "Hey, stowaway! You better not hitch a ride with old Archie here, 'cause I'm herding this tin goose north to the Territories, where if the timber wolves don't eat you, the mosquitoes and black flies will."

The pilot's chuckle blended with laughter outside the plane.

David shivered. He wanted to see orange trees, not icebergs. He considered calling out to the pilot, but couldn't quite face the embarrassment of being turned in, and the words stayed unborn in his throat. Suddenly the right engine growled into life, sputtered, and caught, and then the left. Now it was too late to change his mind.

Moments later the plane rumbled out to the edge of the runway, and as the pilot made one final check of his instruments before takeoff, he radioed ground control for taxiing instructions. "Edmonton Ground Control, this is Grumman 143 listening on 123.6 for taxi instructions for takeoff. Over."

"Grumman 143, proceed to east end of Runway Two." A burst of static filled the cabin, then came the pilot's voice again.

"Edmonton Flight Service Station, this is Grumman 143 listening on 123.6. Advise on weather Edmonton to Fort Smith and Yellowknife. Over."

"Grumman 143, weather clear to Fort Smith and Yellowknife. Possible afternoon turbulence over Wood Buffalo Park. Over."

The plane stopped as the pilot radioed the tower.

"Edmonton Tower, this is Grumman 143 listening on 123.6. On east end of Runway Two. Request permission for takeoff. Over."

More static, then the tower cut in, "Grumman 143, cleared for takeoff. Over."

For some minutes the pilot held the plane at the end of the runway as he gunned first one engine, then the other.

"Grumman 143," the tower cut in, "you are cleared for takeoff. Do you read me? Over."

"Grumman 143 to Tower. I read you loud and clear. Over and out."

"Damn!" the pilot muttered as he clicked off the radio. "I just ain't ready to fly this bird. That port engine oil gauge has got the jitters, and I promised the President I'd be careful with his airplane." He gave the instrument panel a resounding smack.

Now, David thought, the plane would return to the hangar for repairs and he'd cut and run, straight across the fields and cow pastures for home.

But just as David made his decision, the pilot decided to chance it. Once more he requested clearance from the tower. With a deafening, vibrating roar the amphibian picked up speed down the runway and clambered into the air.

Once the craft was airborne and the pilot busy with his controls, David crept out of the hold and took a seat by the window in midplane, hidden from the pilot's view by a bulkhead behind the cockpit.

Beneath the plane the flat, open farmland soon gave way to rolling hills covered with white-barked aspen, bursting with new leaf, with only occasional burned-out clearings, where some hardy young farmer, like Kise in his youth, had tried to wrest a few sections of heavy clay land from the reluctant forest.

Hour after hour the plane droned northward. David kept his nose pressed to the cool window, staring down at a progression of forested hills, and the shining, silver skeins of rivers in spring flood. Once as the plane skimmed low over a lake still frozen on a north hillside, a family of gray wolves caught out on the ice panicked on the slippery surface as they tried to run to shore. Their feet went out from under them and they fell, slipping and sliding as the shadow of the plane raced them down. In spite of caution David giggled aloud, then covered his mouth, thankful that the pilot had not heard him above the roar of the engines.

Gradually the aspen parklands became mixed with birches and black spruces. Here and there he saw marshy clearings of mossy muskeg, dotted with herds of wild wood buffaloes. Great shaggy bulls, still in tattered winter greatcoats, lazed apart, soaking up the weak northern sun while tiny cinnamon-brown calves, newborn and wobbly, pressed close to the sides of their massive mothers as protection from lurking wolves. Remembering his schoolbooks, David guessed that they were flying over Wood Buffalo Park, the largest national park in the world.

Soon, below him, he saw the long jewel of a northern lake, surrounded by the gloom of dense spruce forests. The water was mirror smooth, as though it had not been melted long enough to wrinkle into waves. A large flock of white-winged ducks took fright at the roar of the engines and skimmed across the lake, half flying, half running on the water, as though too heavy to get airborne.

Minutes later David heard the pilot request permission to land at Fort Smith. As the plane lost elevation and circled for a landing, he moved back to the cargo hold. The wheels bumped the runway, the amphibian came to a halt, and the pilot opened the windows and door; then moved out to stand on the wing, David felt a gust of cool air sweep through the plane. From outside the aircraft came the rumble of a fuel truck; the truck door slammed, and a pump began to whine.

"I'd better check the oil while you're fueling her up," the pilot said. "Had trouble with the starboard gauge leaving Edmonton, and I've got some tough flying ahead."

"Where you headed?" the fuel man asked.

"North of Great Slave Lake to count ducks and geese on the breeding grounds. I'll pick up an observer in Yellowknife."

"That's way up there," the voice said. "One thing about it, though, if you get forced down, the walk home ain't crowded."

When the man had finished topping off the tanks, the pilot checked the starboard engine for trouble, but found nothing visibly wrong. Soon the truck rumbled off and all was silent. Apparently the pilot had gone in the truck to get a bite to eat and to pay for the fuel.

It was time for David to make good his escape. He stood at the door, taking in the lay of the land. Near the runway he could see a man operating a bulldozer, but hoped he would be too busy to notice him. Once he had gained the brush, he could easily stay out of sight until he reached Fort Smith, not far distant.

He was ready to step out on the wing when a sharp hammering from the roof and a burst of guttural laughter sent David diving headfirst into the hold. He heard a voice he took to be the dialect of an Indian or an Eskimo, harsh and incomprehensible. For long minutes he lay quiet, listening intently. Then as he took courage from the silence and peered out, he was startled to see a giant raven sitting on the roof. As though in greeting, the raven glided down to the wing, where he strutted back and forth, croaking to his reflection in the shiny aluminum and hammering at the plane's rivets as though to tear them out with his outsize beak.

David had wasted valuable minutes. Now as he moved to leave the plane, he saw it was already too late. The pilot was on his way back.

He had scarcely time to hide before the man stepped up onto the wing and entered. In one hand he held a bag and the plane was filled with the fragrance of hamburgers and onions. Suddenly David felt ravenous. He had been saving his last candy bar for an emergency, but once the plane was airborne, he took it out and munched slowly, making sure no crumb escaped. Except for the clothes on his back and a tattered comic book, he was devouring the last of his worldly possessions.

Four

AS the Grumman Goose droned higher over the Northwest Territories, the air grew colder. Trying desperately to warm himself, David hugged his thin jacket to his body. Tears streamed down his face as fright overwhelmed him. "I want to go home, Kise," he moaned. "I'll be good, I promise. I just want to go back to the farm."

His words were lost in the rumbling roar of the aircraft. He felt a faint whisper of warm air wafting back from the cockpit heater, and he edged up the aisle toward its source. His legs felt numb, and his fingers ached as he blew on them to keep them from freezing.

He envied the pilot his heavy leather jacket with curls of fleece showing at the collar. Creeping closer, he stared over the man's shoulder, fascinated by the bewildering welter of instruments.

Suddenly the plane lurched wildly. From somewhere in the fuselage, metal groaned against metal. His legs buckled, and he clawed the smooth wall for support, but before he could regain his balance, another wild, vicious pitch of the aircraft tumbled him forward into the cockpit.

The pilot stared down at him, while he fought to get his craft back under control.

"What in the name of hell are you doing on my plane?" His heavy hand grabbed David's collar, jerked him upright and flung him into the empty seat.

Perhaps the obvious anguish on David's face helped dissolve the man's anger. He flipped a switch, which sent a flood of warm air in David's direction. "Better snuggle up to that heater, boy. Cold enough back there in that cargo area to freeze the horns off a brass musk ox. If you've been hiding there since Edmonton, it's a wonder you can still walk."

"I figured you were heading for the States," David ventured, "and I could hook a ride without anyone knowing."

"You should have stayed home, kid. However tough things were you should have stuck it out. I got no use for runaways—was one myself. When I finally went home to find the folks, they were dead. I could land this tub in all the whisky I've drunk since, feeling sorry."

"I can do lots of things to help," David pleaded.

The natural twinkle in the pilot's eyes faded. He nodded to the turn indicator, which already showed a shift in the plane's direction. "Sorry, kid. If this were my aircraft I'd give you a ride, even take you north with me for company, but I've got a set of regulations big enough to constipate a mule. All I can do is take you back to Fort Smith. If you want to make a break for it there, you can, but I'd sure advise you to go back to your folks."

He held his hand out to the boy. "Incidentally, my name is Archie."

"Mine's David." He stared ahead at the horizon, feeling almost comfortable in the bath of warm air sweeping by him. Some of the circulation was coming back to his fingers and toes, and with it his resolve. At Fort Smith he'd make a break for it. The pilot looked heavy on his feet and out of condition; it should be easy to outrun him.

Another lurch of the plane took his breath away.

"Look at those thunderheads, would you," Archie growled. "We could try to go through them but I reckon we'd best try to go around."

He banked the plane and headed south, but the scudding clouds seemed to pursue them. Within moments the clouds had engulfed the plane. Lightning split the skies and thunder shook the fuselage. "Check your seat belt, David. I'm going to try to find some flying room beneath the storm, and it may be rough."

A bolt of lightning struck so close in front of them that for a moment both of them were nearly blind.

"There's the ground down there," Archie said in evident relief as he pointed through a gap in the mists. "Looks like there's a few hundred yards' visibility, at least. Better than none at all."

Beneath them David saw a vast, lonely land of stunted spruce, birch, willow, and tamarack, broken by shallow, irregular ponds and mossy marshes—called muskegs—bottomed with permafrost. As far as the eye could see, the land was flat and featureless. What few rivers meandered across the land seemed undecided as to their course and were choked with beaver dams and floating log debris. He wondered how birds flying north could find their way (unerringly) back to the same nesting pond of the previous year, when to him one grassy pond seemed just like the next.

The pilot seemed lost in his own world. He busied himself with his controls, watching the clouds for a break in the weather and alert for a sudden hill rising up from the mists to bat them down.

Ahead of them lightning still battered the landscape and driving rain beat against the windshield, seeping in under the window seal and dripping down David's leg. Now and again drifting patches of fog engulfed them, blotting out the world; at other times the cloud cover seemed to sink, intent on forcing the plane closer and closer to the treetops.

"No good down here," Archie muttered. "Maybe we should try upstairs again, up and over the storm."

He glanced about as if taking one last look at the earth before heading up through the clouds, then suddenly, as he stared past David at the bleak, rain-sodden expanse, he stiffened. "Kid," he said, touching David's arm with a pair of binoculars. "Take a quick look over there in the middle of that pond with these cheaters. No! Way over beyond that line of dead spruces. Just past that tree with the clump on top that looks like an owl watching the marsh. There's something white that doesn't look quite right for a patch of snow."

Grasping the glasses, David peered out over the racing panorama of marshes. He caught a blur of white, lost it, caught it again, and finally brought it into sharp focus. "It's a big white bird, like a swan," he said, "but with black wing tips, and it's stretched out on a floating island as though on a nest."

"It couldn't be!" The pilot's red face darkened with excitement. "We must be three hundred miles from the Sass River area in Wood Buffalo, where the whooping cranes go. I've been flying this north country for many a year and never managed to see a single whooper, let alone find a nest. Those armchair biologists in the home office would give their eye teeth to be in our shoes!" In his excitement the pilot seemed to forget the storm and banked the plane, rubbing one wing against the belly of the clouds to keep from losing sight of the nesting area.

"Is the whooping crane rare?" David asked.

"Rare? You can bet your sweet grandmother's girdle it's rare. When I first heard about whoopers there were only fourteen in existence. They built up some, but bad years hit and the number declined all over again. Last report I had there were only forty-three."

Once more David caught the nest in his view. "Gosh, I hate to tell you then. It looks to me as though the bird on the nest is dead. One wing is stretched out in a funny way, and the head and neck are in the water."

"Dead? You sure, kid?" Archie looked crushed. He stood the big amphibian almost on one wing as he swung the plane about for one more run.

"Sorry, David," Archie apologized, "but I'm going to come in low for a closer look. If it's worth a ground investigation, I'll radio Fort Smith. The Canadian Wildlife Service has a biologist stationed there, and once the storm breaks he can get a helicopter to land him at the site."

As the pilot leveled the aircraft, David saw the ground racing by, and up ahead a bank of clouds threatening to obscure even the trees. Fresh gushets of rain pounded the windowpanes.

The pilot stared ahead, watching for the white apparition on the marshes. David's attention was suddenly caught by a tiny stream of dirty gray oil seeping from the rivets of the engine cowling. Before he could really focus his eyes on it, the oil was swept away by the slip-stream. No! There it was again. A whole line of rivets bleeding oil, the lifeblood of the engine.

"Archie! Look quick!" He touched the pilot on the arm, but Archie was staring hard at his instrument panel, where a needle gauge danced madly. He slapped the panel with his beefy fist, then seemed to notice the stream of oil for the first time.

Swiftly he cut off the port engine. "Don't worry, boy. We can make it home on one."

He had scarcely uttered the words when a violent explosion rocked the plane. Huge streamers of black smoke feathered back from a gaping wound in the wing where the engine had been. On the pilot's side the lone engine roared and shuddered.

"Jerk your seat belt tight and put your face on your knees! Hands on the back of your head!" the pilot roared at David.

David did as he ordered. He felt the roughness of his trousers against his forehead. He thought suddenly of the farm, of the old work team, and he heard again the sudden joyous baying of Speck and Melinda. As the aircraft slued, he stole a quick glance out his window and caught the sight of spruce trees and water spinning into a blur.

"Sorry, kid!" The pilot grabbed for his radio mike, but as he shouted "Mayday! Mayday!" the instrument spun from his hand and shattered against the dash.

The last thing David remembered was the wild scream of shearing metal and a crashing jolt that flung him forward against his seat belt.

Five

FOR a long time David lay listening to the sounds of redwing blackbirds in full spring chorus. Blackbirds usually kept to the marshy bottoms and he couldn't understand why they were so close to the farmhouse. He ached all over. Perhaps he was down in the willow swamp and had fallen out of his tree house.

"Got to get up," he thought, "or Kise will be mad. Got to get up and feed the chickens and get old Parsnip in from the pasture. Got to split Kise some kindling, feed Speck and Melinda, check those new kittens under the barn, and harness the team." He heard what sounded like a flicker drumming on the tin roof of the old slaughterhouse, but when he opened his eyes, the noise wasn't coming from the farm at all but from a loose fragment of metal banging in the wind against what looked as though it had once been the instrument panel of an airplane.

He thought maybe he was dead, and as a man's face began to materialize close by, he wondered if possibly God could have a red face, jug-handled ears, and two black eyes and need a shave. He moved his head until the pain in his neck became unbearable. Someone had dragged him onto a patch of moss and covered him with a leather jacket. God maybe, or whoever that was watching him. "About Kise, God," he said just in case. "It's just ma being gone, I guess, that makes him get mad at me." The man spoke then and the voice jolted him into reality. He remembered the crash.

"You all right, kid?" Archie asked, smiling down at him. "Maybe we'd better shoot that landing all over again. That one was a little rough."

David tried his best to grin and forced himself up on one elbow.

The pilot checked him over for broken bones and poured alcohol from a first-aid kit on the skinned places. Nothing seemed busted but everything hurt.

Slowly, painfully, he crawled to his feet and looked about him. The wreckage lay scattered on the brushy shore of the whooping crane pond which was surrounded by low, scrubby forests and open sphagnum bogs. Some distance away, out on a marshy section of the pond, he could see the body of the whooping crane, like a remnant drift of winter snow in the middle of the tree-ringed water. A pale sun shone through thin clouds.

"I'm sure glad you're awake," Archie said. "You've been out cold for a couple of hours, but talking all sorts of nonsense."

"You hurt, Archie?" David asked, then felt foolish when he saw that the pilot had fashioned a crude splint for his leg and bound it securely with rags.

"Busted," the man said, then, as though to relieve the boy of worry, he added, "I'm a tough old coot. It'll heal."

The plane was a shambles. In shearing off a clump of trees at the edge of the pond both wings and the rear section had broken away, though the nose and part of the cargo area remained intact but battered. David realized that the pilot's skill in keeping the plane aloft until the last possible second, and the fact that the landing site happened to be covered with a two-foot cushion of sphagnum moss, had undoubtedly saved their lives.

"What about the radio?" David asked hopefully.

"Out for good," the pilot said. "I think my knee went through it. We'll just have to sweat it out until they find us." Just who "they" were he made no effort to explain. He limped to the wreckage, reached in through a gaping hole in the cabin, and drew out a paper bag. "I've got a hamburger left," he said to David. "I got it in Fort Smith. You'd better eat it. It might be quite a ways to the next restaurant."

"You eat it," David said. "It's yours."

"Nah, kid. They made a mistake at the airport café. They know I don't like onions."

The meat was cold and the bun stale, but David wolfed it down. If he sensed that the pilot was tense and worried, maybe even a little afraid, David himself viewed his surroundings with a growing calm. Kise had often taken him north of Edmonton for long camping trips in the woods and taught him all manner of useful lore. Kise had bragged to his friend Elmore Claridge that it was like pulling hen's teeth to get "that boy" out of the woods and home again.

David examined what was left of the fuselage. With a little work it would be a passable shelter against any future rainstorm. Walking gingerly over the shards of twisted metal that littered the cockpit area, he poked his head up through a gaping hole in the roof. From atop a dead spruce at the edge of the water a northern water thrush was singing its heart out. Some might have taken it for a love song, but David knew the bird was only warning others away from his nesting territory. In the scrub willows warblers were courting, and on the lake a male bufflehead was rushing back and forth trying to choose between two females, both of whom ignored his antics. In spite of all that had happened to him, David was caught up by the beat of excitement in the air.

From his perch atop the wreckage he glanced down to see Archie fashioning a crutch from a small spruce sheared and split from the impact. David's own leg began to ache in sympathy. "Better rest," David chided as he crawled down out of the fuselage. He moved slowly; his muscles were beginning to stiffen and cramp.

Archie continued to work at his crutch. "I'm worried about that whooping crane," he said. "Maybe the incubating crane hasn't been dead all that long and there's still life left in the eggs. If we could save a whooping crane or two by hatching them out, why, I reckon that would be a whole lot more important than hurting this leg. When a species dies out to that degree, every bit of blood is important to the race." Pulling himself to his feet, Archie tested his crutch and made one faltering step toward the pond. His face went gray with pain.

David stared at Archie in wonderment. With a broken leg he had no chance of wading to the nest. He'd either drown by stumbling in the muck or by fainting from sheer pain. Why would a grownup care that much about a bird? A whooping crane must really be special.

"Getting the eggs will take some doing," David said. "All I've got is some sore muscles; I should be the one to go."

Archie's jaw set stubbornly, but the next step he made toward the pond made him reel with pain.

"All right then, but be careful," he warned. "Don't go deeper than you can wade or you'll get cramps and drown. And if you manage to get the eggs, be sure you don't crack them."

David removed his boots and left them near the plane, then walked gingerly through strewn wreckage down toward the water's edge. Slowly, painfully, he limped along the shore until he reached the point of land nearest the nest.

The water was the color of Kise's morning coffee, and spooky. As he stepped in, the bottom marl squished through his toes. The skinned places on his shins stung, but soon the cold snow water numbed his legs so that he had little feeling left. Timid at first, he waded close to shore, then gradually, as he grew confident that no great monster of the north was going to rise out of the murk to gobble him up, he ventured farther and farther into the gloomy marsh.

Something slimy bumped against his thighs, and he almost turned and rushed for shore. The water rose to his waist. A blackbird perched on the crane as though it were no more than a stump, but flew off scolding as David approached. A sadness swept over him when he saw how beautiful the big bird looked even in death. Rippling the pond, a light wind teased her plumes, making her seem almost alive.

Her long black legs were tucked beneath her, and one wing was still half folded at her side. The water was devoid of vegetation around the nest, where she had pulled up the emergent rushes to build her island.

Softly, as though in fear of waking her, David searched beneath her breast. His heart sank as he found broken fragments of shell sticking to her feathers. Then suddenly his fingers closed about an egg. Carefully he drew it out into the light. Larger than that of a goose, it almost covered his palm. His own body chilled from the cold waters of the lake,

his teeth chattering, he felt its warmth by contrast. Perhaps the embryo inside was still alive. For a moment the boy rested his free hand on the old crane's back. "I'll take good care of your last egg," he said. "I promise."

Just as David turned from the nest to head back to shore, he heard a loud, angry trumpeting. Over the spruces and tamaracks swept a huge male whooping crane, wings outstretched, landing gear down. The lad gasped at the seven-foot wingspread; he saw the red and black markings of the head, the great yellow eyes, and the formidable black and yellow beak. The crane landed at the edge of the pond, waded out a few short steps, then, as he saw David, called out in alarm, tipping his beak to the sky. "Kerloo! Kerloo!" he bugled. Next, pretending injury, he did a broken-wing act, attempting to lure David into following and leaving the nest unharmed.

For a moment David felt a flash of shame that he had taken the egg, then reason prevailed. Without a quick supply of heat to revive the embryo, the egg would be doomed. And so he waded on, fearful lest he stumble and lose the future of the whooping crane race in the murky waters.

For some time the crane stood at the edge of the pond, as though he sensed that the eggs were gone. Then, without sound or fanfare, he turned, ran a few steps into the wind, lifted into the air, and with slow, majestic wing beats, cleared the tops of the trees and disappeared.

The breeze rippling the pond was chill, and as

David waded, he placed the egg next to his skin for warmth and hugged his jacket tight about it. It suddenly occurred to the boy that getting the egg was one thing; keeping it warm, yet not too warm, was another.

Archie sat waiting for him at the edge of the camp. "You've got them," he said, eyeing the bulge in David's jacket.

"Just one," David replied. "The other was broken."

Archie stared at the treasure cupped in David's hands. "Now comes the real challenge," he said. "We've no thermometer to gauge temperatures and too little heat is as bad as too much. Body temperature would be about right, while the campfire might cook it rather than hatch it."

"You're the expert on whooping cranes," David said. "You hatch the egg. Besides, that way you'll take care of your leg. Me, I'll gather the food and do any other chores you want me to do."

"But—" Archie protested.

"The egg," David said firmly, handing it to him, "is getting cold."

"I'll be blamed if I'll sit around doing nothing," Archie said. "If planes come over the area we've got to be ready to attract their attention. Thanks to the storm, we're way off the course I filed in my flight plan. They'll check out that route the moment they discover I didn't arrive in Yellowknife to pick up an observer. Then, if they don't assume I sank the plane in Great Slave Lake, they may search out other areas. These trees might look sparse to us on the ground, but they pretty well screen the wreckage from any but direct flights overhead. We've got to pack shiny pieces of metal down to the shore, make an SOS visible from the air, then lay up some piles of dry brush so that fires can be lighted in a hurry if any planes show."

"The egg," David reminded him. "I'll do the rest." With the pilot muttering under his breath, David took a slab of sheet metal from the wreck, lined it with soft sphagnum moss, helped Archie into this makeshift bed, and covered him with a blanket of canvas. When the boy finally left to do his chores, the American was resting quietly with the whooping crane egg nestled snugly in a nest of dry moss against the fever-warm skin of his fat belly.

Six

GUIDED by Archie, David picked up pieces of aluminum from the fuselage, packed them down to the shore of the lake, and placed them to form an SOS visible from the air. The completion of a signal made them both feel better.

Ferreting about in the wreckage, the boy found a small sheet of cardboard, which he folded into a crude cornucopia in which to gather food. With this under his arm he limped along the shores of the neighboring marshes, looking for any food that might keep them alive. He had in mind finding some tule roots or sweet buds of cattails, which Kise had told him were delicious, but he was farther north than he had imagined and either they did not exist or had not yet emerged from the cold May waters, so recently bound in ice.

His whole afternoon gathering consisted of a few handfuls of last year's crowberries, some dandelion leaves from a southern exposure, and a quart of tiny freshwater snails, which clung in huge numbers to sunken logs.

Fox tracks were everywhere and David had the feeling that wherever he went the foxes had already been there, sniffing out all the available food. Still, their presence gave him hope. Kise had always maintained that where there were foxes in the north there were apt to be lots of arctic hares.

Returning to camp with his loot, he tried to remove the tiny snails from their shells, but soon he gave up, took two flat stones, and, Indian style, smashed shells and all into a pulp, adding greens and berries to the mess. Though the concoction looked about as appetizing as a mouthful of wet sand he built up the fire and propped a crude container of sheet aluminum against some rocks to simmer the raw food into stew.

One of his chores when Kise had taken him camping had been to provide new meat for the pot of rabbit stew Kise liked to keep at a simmer on the campfire. This was one way, perhaps, to show Archie that he could carry his part of the load. Back in the brush David located the more fragmented of the plane's wings. Working quietly so as not to disturb Archie, he pried back some of the aluminum to expose the bundles of insulated copper wire, which had led to the running lights on the wing. By placing the wire against the edge of a sharp rock and using a blunt stone as a hammer, he soon cut it into two-foot lengths. Taking each length separately, he put a slip loop in one end, and made a bundle of colorful, but effective, snares.

As he passed through the camp on his way to hunt, he added fuel to the fire and saw that the pilot still slumbered peacefully, the egg cradled against his chest. He knew the egg would be safe from crushing because Archie could not turn over without waking from the pain.

Once he had gained the woods, he worked his way slowly and carefully, establishing a trail by breaking spruce boughs and letting them hang to mark his passage. In this flat land there were no landmarks and he knew that he must be painstakingly careful not to lose his way. "The north gives you just one chance," Kise had said once. "Remember, boy, it's no place for a fool."

Here and there as he walked he found piles of white feathers where a fox had dined on ptarmigan, plump little "arctic chickens," but since none of the kills showed the brown plumage of summer, David guessed that with the melting of snows, the birds had moved north to the barrens to nest and would not return until autumn.

It was far easier to catch hares with snow on the ground. Then they kept to well-packed trails, and once you had found an established run, it was only a matter of time before the animal came bobbing down the same highway again. But now the snow lay only in a few scattered patches of dirty slush hidden deep in the densest thickets, and signs were hard to read.

But soon his sharp eyes detected where hares had been nibbling on greens. Breaking off dead canes from scrub willows, David made low fences through the brush, leaving a gap in each fence just wide enough for a hare to squeeze through. In each of these gates he set a wire loop, fastening the free end to a nearby sapling, so that when the quarry came by, the noose would slip tight about its neck and the end would come swiftly.

Overhead gray jays followed him from tree to tree, as though curious about what he was up to. David had a feeling they were spying out his sets and would warn all the hares in the forest.

When he had finished, he followed his trail back to camp and found the pilot sitting by the fire with the big brown egg exposed to the chill air.

Archie saw his alarm and grinned. "It's safe, David. As an egg cools, it draws in oxygen through the shell and keeps the chick healthy. The whooping cranes would approve." He nodded toward the snail stew. "You're a great cook! Whatever you put into that stew was a little gritty, but it tastes delicious."

David helped himself, secretly proud to have pleased the old pilot. Any squeamishness he might have felt at tasting the stew was quickly overcome by his ravenous appetite, and the hot liquid seemed as good and as nourishing as any Kise had ever made.

Once he had devoured all but the sand in the bottom of the crude pot, he set about making the camp more comfortable.

As David gathered fresh moss and boughs for their beds, Archie seemed to forget his pain. Smoking the last of his cigars, he cradled the egg tenderly.

"Reckon it's alive at that," he said. "It seems to generate some of its own heat and stay warm exposed to the air. An egg with a dead embryo would cool off fast. Maybe I'm dreaming," Archie went on, "but sometimes I even sense movement inside the egg."

For some minutes they rested in silence. Then suddenly Archie put out his cigar and sat listening as though he heard aircraft in the distance.

"Hear that, kid?" he boomed. "Told you they'd come looking for old Archie!"

David jumped to his feet and for long minutes stood listening, but sadly the only sounds he could detect were the voices of far-off winds, sweeping over the scrubby arctic forests. "Sorry, David," the man said quietly.

That night they both took their turns incubating the whooping crane egg. It was unusually cold, and twice David had to go out into the gloomy half-light of the arctic night to gather more moss to heap over their bodies as a blanket. Now and again the boy was awakened by fevered groans and curses from the pilot, and knew that his friend was in pain.

By morning the last vestiges of the storm front had blown away and the sun shone from a faultless sky to warm the land. Awakening to a chorus of bird song,

David dragged himself from his bed, built up the fire, washed himself in the icy pond, and went off to check his snares.

Not far from camp he found a duck's nest hidden in a patch of bog myrtle. Since the duck had not yet lined her nest with down, he knew she had not yet started incubation. Once he would never have dreamed of stealing eggs, but hunger makes its own morals. The hen would have to lay another clutch; this one would go toward nursing Archie back to health.

When David approached his first snare, his heart skipped a beat. He had caught a hare but only a few bits of fur remained. There in the soft mud were giant pad marks where a timber wolf, checking out the boy's trail, had caught a succulent dinner without even trying. A gray jay laughed harshly from a treetop as though it were he who had led the wolf to the set.

In the next set David found a dead hare. Its fur was tattered since this was the time of year when hares traded their white coats for the brown vestments of summer. Breaking the thin skin along the back with his strong fingers, as he had done so often in the past for Kise, he jerked off the skin as though it were a sweater and trousers two sizes too large. Leaving the internal organs as homage to the foxes, he picked a salad of fresh dandelion greens and early duckweed, then headed in triumph back to camp.

Archie shook his head in wonder as he saw the eggs and the hare. "Kid, you're really something, you are.

Here I am lying around camp feeling sorry for myself and you come in with groceries."

David tried his best to suppress a grin of satisfaction. But as he busied himself around camp he found himself thinking about Kise, wishing he were here. Much as he'd done so far, Kise would have done more. By now, even without an axe, Kise would have had a crude, but snug, shelter thrown up against any unexpected late spring storms; even without a gun, he'd have managed a bull moose hanging up in camp for meat. Kise was a careful man and always one to find a way. David was beginning to understand that the fact that Kise had been a strict, demanding taskmaster and drilled him in woodsmanship might now make the difference between death or survival.

That evening when the chores were done, David helped the pilot from his bed to a seat before the campfire while they let the egg cool in the evening air. Archie smoked his last cigar with deliberation. The day before, he had smoked half of it, and now it was rank and bitter. He almost scorched his lips trying to make it last. "Know what I'm about to give up?" he asked. "Coffee, cigars, whisky, and women."

"And flying airplanes," David added.

"Especially Air Force Number Two here," Archie grinned. "You may not believe this but actually I'm a pretty good pilot."

Once they had dined on stew, duck eggs, and greens boiled up like spinach, Archie tossed his hat on a nearby tree limb and stretched out on the couch David had built him by the fire to soak up heat into his aching leg. "Relax, kid," he said. "You've been hard at it all day. Makes me worn out just to watch you."

"I've got things to do," David replied. With a wedge of steel from the plane, he split a five-foot birch log into staves until he found one with a straight grain that suited him. Then, with a piece of broken glass, he sat by the fire and scraped away at the wood until he had fashioned a crude bow. Often as he worked he paused to bend each arm of the bow to make it more limber and less apt to shatter. When the weapon was finished, he garnered some more wire from the wreck to use as a bow string. The Indians, he acknowleged to Archie, had never had it so good.

From the brush bordering the camp he cut his arrow stock, feathering each bolt with ptarmigan feathers gathered from old fox kills and bound to the shaft with fine wire; the points he sharpened with Archie's knife and hardened with repeated charrings in the fire.

Archie had his first real laugh of the day when he saw the finished product. "What on earth are you going to shoot with that contraption? A moose?"

"The moose comes later," David replied. "After I practice. Right now I'm after grouse. I found a grouse feather today in a thicket and early this evening I thought I heard one drum."

Archie snorted. "Come on now, kid. I've seen grouse fly. You couldn't even hit my hat hanging on that dead limb."

David bridled at the teasing. Calmly he drew back

an arrow and let fly. The hat spun crazily into the air and almost dropped into the fire near Archie's feet.

"Well, I'll be—!" Archie exclaimed, putting his fingers through a hole in the crown of his hat. "If we ever have a war, I hope I'm on your side."

As David retrieved his arrow, a light spatter of rain put an end to their jesting. "That's the north country for you," Archie grumbled. "One minute sun, the next rain."

As the campfire sizzled and spat indignantly, David helped Archie into the shelter of the plane fuselage. They entered just in time, for the clouds seemed to open up to drench them in an icy torrent.

Soon the campfire was reduced to a wisp of steam, and water cascaded down on their mossy beds through gaping holes in the roof. "I'd go fix the roof," Archie muttered, "but my hat's got a hole in it."

With the sun obscured, the temperature dropped forty degrees to just above freezing. Now and again the rain was mixed with large wet flakes of snow. David hunched his shoulders against the downpour, and went out to salvage aluminum sheeting from the tail section. Working quickly, he soon covered the major holes with metal weighted down with large rocks. From one wing section he managed a large sheet, which made a wall for the fuselage where the tail section had been sheared away.

By now his fingers were wet and numb, and his teeth chattering. He had a choice of shivering through the night or improvising a stove. From the wreckage he extracted a five-gallon tin, which had previously been ignored since it had suffered such damage in the crash as to make it useless for holding water. Now, with Archie's knife he cut a hole in one end for a door and another beneath the door for a draft, and set the contraption on a layer of rocks on the floor of the hut. Next he rolled pieces of aluminum into a stovepipe, fitted them together, inserted one end in the top of the can and the other through a hole in the roof, and the stove was finished.

Gathering handfuls of dead spruce needles from protected areas beneath trees, he soon had a crackling fire; wind was whistling through the draft, and the whole stove turned such a lovely cherry-red that Archie had to move to the far side of his bed for fear of overheating the incubating egg. "Hey, this is great," Archie said. "Think I'll stay home from bowling tonight and watch television."

For three days the cold rains battered them. David managed one trip to his snares, but they had been beaten down by the onslaught, and besides, in such weather all self-respecting hares were keeping to their beds. And so snails and a few dandelion greens constituted their fare.

It was a difficult time for the injured man. Not only did his leg ache in the damp air, but the natural restlessness of his nature made it hard for him to lie still and serve as an incubator. Once the storm had blown itself out and the skies cleared, Archie moved back outdoors and spent much of his time watching for planes.

One morning as David was cooking some duck

eggs at the fire, Archie shouted suddenly in great excitement. "Quick, kid. Grab my shaving mirror. There's a big jet way high, a terrible long shot, but we'd better try."

David saw the long, thin contrails pluming the sky. Archie manipulated the mirror, but they had no way of knowing if the flashes were even visible.

The plane passed out of sight. "Most likely every one of those passengers had his nose in a magazine and wouldn't report the flashes to the pilot if he saw them," Archie grumbled.

Two days later they saw another jet plane cruising high and lighted a huge signal fire, but the persistent winds scattered the smoke, and they were left more discouraged than before. "It's all right, David boy," Archie said, touching him on the arm. "They missed that signal, but one of these days they'll read us and come swarming. It just takes time."

Even if no one came to their aid, one situation improved markedly and that was the food supply. David found a ruffed grouse feeding along a game trail and before the bird could even fly managed a quick shot with an arrow and scored. In his snares that morning he beat the wolves to not one hare but four of them.

Archie was delighted but puzzled. "Too bad we don't have refrigeration. It would be a shame to let any of that meat spoil."

David ducked his head to hide a sly grin. For some hours Archie heard a racket in the brush over by the tail section as though David were building a new plane with a stone hammer. Soon the boy emerged from the trees, carrying a contraption that looked like a miniature outhouse.

"A smokehouse!" Archie exclaimed. David nodded and set about cutting their extra meat into thin strips, which he hung on wires in the little house to cure over a willow fire.

But David's triumph was short-lived. At dawn the next day they were roused by a loud crash and looked up from their beds to see a huge black bear cannonading off through the brush with half the smokehouse hanging from its neck.

Tears of discouragement welled in David's eyes as he saw what havoc had been wrought, but suddenly he was aware that the strangulated sounds coming from Archie's bed were of laughter and not pain, and soon the boy too managed to smile.

Profiting by the adventure, he built another smokehouse, but this time he invented a distant early-warning system, consisting of a trip wire passing from tree to tree all about the circumference of the camp. This would warn them of an intruder by collapsing a stack of aluminum sheets in thunderous alarm.

The pair of wolves that laid claim to this territory and sometimes robbed his snares were silent during this season of the year, for they were busy raising young. If David caught sight of them at all it was only as a distant shadow in the bush, gone almost before his eyes could focus. Soon, however, he found their den in a gravel bank a mile or so from camp, and whenever he found time, he liked to watch the pups as they wrestled and played in front of their burrow.

Often he took waste scraps of meat and bones to the den for the pups, and soon they crowded around the entrance of their burrow to see what new delicacy he had to offer.

One day as David returned to camp from feeding the pups, swinging a brace of hares he had killed with arrows, he was startled to see that Archie was doubled up on his couch by the fire as though in great pain, both hands clutching his stomach.

Forgetting the alarm system, David charged toward the camp, sending sheets of aluminum crashing in pandemonium. "Archie!" he shouted above the din. "You OK?"

"Quick!" Archie gasped. "Go boil some water. I'm about to become a mother!"

From inside the shell of the whooping crane egg came a whistling, plaintive "preep!"

Seven

IT was one of those mornings when the whole northland seemed to come alive at once. A soft, balmy wind sent songbirds warbling and fighting over territories; white-winged crossbills sang from the tops of budding tamaracks; gray jays, or "whisky jacks," perched jauntily on the wreckage, awaiting scraps of food. The first tree swallows descended in a cloud to skim the marshes for insects or to take their pick of choice nesting holes in trees.

Drumming his cheery good morning on the aluminum fuselage, a yellow-shafted flicker leaped in astonishment and retreated to the neighboring forest as though he hadn't intended to make half that much noise. Showering the ground with chips, a pair of northern three-toed woodpeckers took turns drilling a fresh nest in a decaying spruce. A pair of gray sand-hill cranes, smaller than whooping cranes, flew low over the camp, so close their rosy crowns shone bright in the morning sun.

Through all this awakening man and boy sat trans-fixed by the tapping sounds that came from the big brown egg cradled against Archie's chest. Nature had provided the whooping crane chick with a temporary little can opener atop his rubbery bill in the form of a sharp ivory egg tooth. Every few minutes, inside the egg, the little head would jerk back spasmodically as with a hiccup, and the egg tooth would strike a blow for freedom, knocking out chip after tiny chip until it had turned full circle and the cap tumbled off like a trap door to reveal the crane and his inner world.

For a long time the rare little bird lay still, resting from his long struggle and seemingly reluctant to leave the safety of his ruptured shell.

"Think we should help?" Archie asked, touching the shell with clumsy forefinger.

"I've watched lots of chickens hatch on the farm. My stepfather, Kise, says always give a chick plenty of time. Way he tells it, the chick gets his food from the yolk sac through tiny veins, which dry up as the sac is absorbed into his body. Help a chick out of the shell too soon, and the veins are liable to rupture and bleed."

Archie withdrew his hand.

Soon, however, the little whooping crane made the

decision for them by kicking off the remnant shell and flopping out of the cradle of Archie's hands into his big lap.

"He's so wet and weak," Archie said. "He can't possibly live."

"Just you wait," retorted David. "He's got to live. Look! He's already holding up his head!"

For a time the gosling-sized newcomer gazed about with dark, uncomprehending eyes, then collapsed on the pilot's lap, where he soon snuggled into the folds of his jacket. For however long they could keep the tiny heart beating, there was one more whooping crane this side of extinction.

That night they took turns baby-sitting before the fire. Attracted by plaintive peeping, a great gray owl glided in on silent wings and perched atop a low spruce, while a fox crept in to see if the new sound in the forest was something good to eat.

Watching the fox, who would have devoured the last whooping crane chick on earth without a twinge of conscience, David realized how awesome was his responsibility to be alert. In one unguarded second a northern goshawk, skimming in low over the land, could dart in from the thickets, seize the chick, and be gone. Stretching his legs, the boy roused the drowsy fire with a kick, put on extra wood, then sat soaking up the new warmth as the crane chick settled comfortably in his lap and Archie punctured the night with snores.

By the third day both Archie and David were exhausted. On thin, uncertain legs the crane tripped over every root, but he refused to stay put. Active and spry, he followed them constantly around camp, piping plaintively as though begging for something neither knew how to give. Whenever David offered him a bug, he rose to his full height of eight inches and refused to accept it.

"Wish he would settle for dandelion greens and snail stew the way we had to," David remarked. He had been hunting in vain for new insects, but outside of a teaspoon of mosquito larvae, he had found nothing.

"If he doesn't take on some groceries soon," Archie said, "he'll die."

"There has to be a food source here, doesn't there?" David asked. "Otherwise the whooping cranes would have picked some other place to nest."

Suddenly the boy thought of the snails. Rushing to the pond, he plucked a large, juicy specimen from a reed near shore, crushed the shell between thumb and forefinger, and offered it to the chick, who had come running along behind and now was regarding every movement with interest. In an instant the tiny bird seized the snail in his rubbery bill and swallowed it.

"Hey, Archie! Come here!" David shouted, forgetting the pilot's broken leg. Dropping on his hands and knees, the boy watched in amazement as the lump proceeded down one side of the neck, then crossed to the other, and disappeared down the gullet, while the crane piped excitedly for more.

Archie's face was ashen from pain when he hobbled up on his crude crutches. This had been his longest excursion away from camp, and he was still far from well. But his thoughts were of the baby crane.

"Snails!" the pilot marveled. "The answer was right here all the time. Right under our noses." Together they fed the eager little bird from their fingertips until he could hold no more.

During the next few days the chick was practically smothered with attention as David and Archie vied with each other. David spent less time hunting and used every possible excuse to return to camp. If it wasn't his arrows that he'd forgotten, it was wire for snares, and he spent much time just sitting before the fire.

The sight of the great male whooping crane on the marsh, the adventures with the egg, and the hatching of the chick had left him with a desire to know more about the species, and he pumped Archie for information.

"What folks don't know about the whooping crane," Archie said, "would fill a washtub. But year by year we're coming to understand the bird better, and someday maybe we'll know enough to help save it from extinction."

"How did you get so interested, Archie?" David asked.

In his huge hands the baby crane dozed contentedly. "I flew some of the early flights searching for the nesting grounds," Archie replied. "You see, until 1952, no one knew where the last of the whooping cranes nested. They would leave Aransas Refuge in late March or early April, fly so high over the land that very few people saw them pass, and simply vanish into this vast mosquito farm up here. In autumn they'd come back with any young they'd managed to raise."

Glancing about him, David could see how even a big, conspicuous bird like a whooping crane could remain hidden, for the ponds were small and encircled by trees, and only a chance overhead flight would reveal the presence of a crane. "I guess," he said to Archie almost sadly, "with thousands of acres of look-alike country there was no more chance of search parties stumbling across the whooping cranes than there is of finding us here."

It was a good observation, but instantly David was sorry he had said it, for on Archie's face David saw the pressures and strains, the shadow of his doubts.

"We've got a good chance," Archie said stubbornly. "Maybe we have been here a couple of weeks. It's a big country, but, after all, they found the whooping crane. That summer of '52 a biologist making water-fowl surveys in a Grumman Goose just like this one saw two of the big birds north of Great Slave. That was a pretty exciting event, but it wasn't until '54 that some fire fighters, returning home by helicopter from a forest fire in a remote section of Wood Buffalo, happened to look down into a glade in time to see two mature birds and their young."

"I'll bet that caused an uproar," David said.

Archie nodded. "The news flashed around the world and captured public interest. For the first time the public began to link the struggle of the whooping crane for survival with their own environmental crises."

As he stared into the fire the pilot smiled. "There were suddenly a lot of experts around, each with a different idea on how to save the whooping crane. Some folks wanted to protect the bird but otherwise leave it strictly alone; others believed in captive management, pointing out that the existing birds were exposed to all sorts of natural disasters, such as the off-season hurricane that wiped out a nonmigratory colony of whoopers in Louisiana in 1941, and that it might be best to move right into a crash program of trying to propagate the species in captivity."

Archie looked at his watch. It was almost midnight, but there was still daylight in this northern land, and both of them were having trouble going to bed, particularly when every bird about them seemed noisily committed to keeping them awake. The pilot yawned suggestively, but David, who was mending some mosquito netting he had found in the wreckage, was still in the mood for conservation.

"Had anyone ever raised a whooping crane in captivity?" he asked.

"Not at that point," Archie admitted. "But just about then two whooping cranes at the Audubon Park Zoo, Crip and Josephine, finally succeeded in producing four young from two clutches of eggs. That strengthened those who thought the birds' future could be insured by captive propagation."

David took the little crane from Archie's hands,

held him a moment, then set him down near the fire. The bird stood for a moment as though enjoying the warmth, but soon moved off to explore the campsite, playing restlessly with twigs and bits of leaf as if searching for food. "I don't understand," David said, "how they ever planned to get enough whooping crane breeding stock. I mean, that's one item you don't buy in a pet store."

"You're right," Archie agreed. "There was just one way they could get stock and that was to gather eggs from wild nests, just the way we did here."

"You mean they stole eggs from the wild birds?"

Archie nodded. "Just flew their helicopters into the nesting areas and stole one egg from each nest. The biologists had observed that while the cranes were laying two eggs and hatching two young, they were generally only raising one of them anyhow. They reasoned that if they stole one egg from each nest to hatch in captivity, the remaining egg would get the undivided attention of both parents, and thus the chick would have a better chance of survival."

The whooping crane chick pecked at an interesting-looking worm, which turned out to be his own middle toe, and fell flat on his back. Like excited bantam hens, Archie and David fluttered to help, but the little bird struggled back up as though nothing had happened. "Preep!" he said and went on poking about the campsite.

Archie hopped back to his seat on a log and David joined him. "Next time take along your crutches," the boy suggested, sensing the pain the man felt.

STRANGE COMPANION

Archie took a stick and began tracing random sketches on the ground. To take his mind off his leg he resumed their conversation about cranes. "It took lots of guts on the part of wildlife officials to decide to steal the eggs," he went on. "If the program had failed, the public would have gotten pretty sore. As it was, the program worked like a charm. They stole the eggs, flew them off by jet aircraft in a heated suitcase to a research center in Maryland, and hatched and raised a good percentage of the chicks. The interesting thing is they've stolen eggs on alternate years ever since, and the years they've gathered eggs the cranes have had far better nesting success. Last season, with no gathering, the cranes laid about twenty-five eggs, yet only made it to Aransas with one chick. More and more, folks are coming to realize that building a captive flock is important. But it will take time for the birds to reach breeding age, and once we have a good annual supply of crane eggs from the flock, we'll have to figure out a way to raise the chicks, not for captivity, but for release into the wild."

"That might be tough," David said. "Does anyone have any suggestions how?"

"Best idea so far seems to be to place the eggs in sandhill crane nests in suitable areas where the sandhill nesting dates most nearly match those of the whoopers."

"Hey," David said. "That might work. The sandhills would raise the young whoopers and teach them whatever a young crane has to know to survive. Like where to find food or how to stay away from danger."

"And how to migrate," Archie said. "Most likely the young whoopers would migrate with the sandhill foster parents and that way come to accept other wintering areas besides the limited coastal areas they use now."

"Sometimes I used to watch the sandhills when they stopped to feed in southern Alberta," David mused. "They're smaller and gray where the whoopers are white."

"Let's hope the plan works. At least it's a better gamble than doing nothing at all." Archie yawned and stretched his arms. "Me for the sack, kid. Better get some shuteye yourself."

"You sleep," he replied, "and I'll baby-sit."

As Archie settled for the night the crane returned from his investigations of the grounds and seemed ready for a midnight snack. David fed him some snails and some fresh rabbit liver, cut into strips, until the crane's piping became less demanding.

David settled by the fire with the little bird on his lap, stroking the soft down along the back of his neck until the bird's dark eyes blinked and closed in sleep. In the forest a great gray owl hooted softly, and he could hear a moose splashing in the pond as it fed on bottom vegetation. The fire collapsed, sending a flurry of light gray ashes into the air, and all was still.

Eight

ARCHIE and David need not have felt neglected by the world as they awaited rescue. Failure of the Goose to touch down at Yellowknife set off a thorough and efficient air search operation along those areas covered by Archie's flight plan, but by the first week in June, when no trace of the big silver amphibian had been found, it was generally assumed that the plane had crashed in the vast gray expanses of Great Slave Lake and that all traces had been blotted out by floating fields of ice. One by one the search planes were recalled for other duties, for the summers in the north are short and busy and every day of good weather is precious.

DAYTON O. HYDE

Had Archie known, he might have had a bit of wry satisfaction from the fact that when a brand new Grumman Goose left Dulles International Airport in Washington, D.C., bound for Yellowknife, his replacement was not one pilot biologist but two. But his ego might have been battered had he known how quickly the world had adapted to his absence and how little it had been changed by those events in the north.

Far to the south, at Aransas Refuge, Captain Bowen had tied his charter boat, "Birdwatcher," to the dock and was utilizing this lull between tourist seasons to overhaul his engines. The pilot who had attempted to follow the migrating cranes as they left Aransas had moved to Mississippi to work at aerial crop dusting with his brother. The Audubon Society biologist had temporarily ceased his studies during the absence of the whoopers to testify in a court battle against further dredging of offshore areas of the refuge by barges mining reefs of oyster shell. The refuge manager himself, now that the celebrity whoopers were no longer in residence, was enjoying his respite, with crises no more serious than an occasional fisherman lost or stranded by the tides.

David too might have had a few sad thoughts had he known that back in Edmonton Kise missed his stepson mightily, but had exhausted all leads in his attempt to trace the boy. After fruitless searches among the communes of runaway youths in neighboring cities, Kise had finally returned to the drudgery of trying to run the farm without David's help.

Meanwhile in the north Archie and David were

busy caring for the whooping crane chick, which had come to be the center of their lives.

One warm, sunny day in mid-June Archie and David sat in camp in attendance upon the young crane.

"What'll we name him?" Archie asked, feeding the bird a snail.

"He's rusty colored," David observed. "Let's call him Rusty." And so the crane was named.

Insatiably curious, Rusty made a playground of the camp, probing each cranny with hardening beak, playing a tug of war with anything tuggable, from boot laces to trouser cuffs, upsetting the wobbly water bucket David had made from sheeting from the wreckage, piping plaintively whenever David or Archie dared divert their attention to some more urgent task, such as preparing a meal for themselves. The slightest movement or interesting noise from either of them brought the crane running for a hand-out.

Walks with David were a special cause for excitement. Rusty began with a scamper and a waving of stubby wings until invariably the chick outdid himself, tripped on a stick, and landed, struggling, flat on his back.

His favorite journey was along the pond, where he waded, probed the soft marl for unseen objects, bathed, sunned, and preened happily or chased after butterflies, never quite catching them in his stubby bill. When David left camp to hunt, Archie had to re-strain Rusty to keep him from chasing off into the dangerous forests. Each time that David returned, the little bird rushed out to greet him and escort him into camp.

One day as Archie and David were both in camp, the little crane, probing with his beak in the wreckage of the nose, pulled out Archie's flight maps and with great delight began to scatter them about camp.

"Hey, you little devil," David cried out, retrieving the maps before they could be scattered by the wind.

Sitting with the boy close beside him, Archie spread out the maps and pored over them, trying to pinpoint their exact location while the little crane ran endless circles around them.

"Way I figure it," Archie said, "we're here." He pointed out a spot on the map to David. "In this direction it's three hundred miles to a road, but eight hundred miles if you make a bad choice and head in the wrong direction. Any way you want to go from here you're going to be hampered by brush, wandering rivers, swamps, insects, and lack of landmarks."

"There's a compass in the wreckage," David said hopefully.

Archie shook his head. "Next to worthless here. Too many underground deposits of iron ore to set the needle off. It would only confuse us, and as for guiding on the sun, this time of year the sun seems nailed in the sky. The last few days we've had no real darkness at all or rising and setting of the sun."

"How about locating a river?" David asked. "Couldn't we find one and raft on down until we come to Great Slave Lake or something?"

Again Archie shook his head. "Look at this map. On this flat land rivers seem to meander forever and are so choked up with beaver dams and fallen timber they're impossible to navigate."

Suddenly Archie raised his head from the map. "Listen!" he said. A faint droning noise almost like that of a distant plane came from the marshy borders of the pond. Archie's face fell. "Mosquitoes," he said. "Their larvae are hatching out and from now on it's going to be hell."

David could see a pair of alder flycatchers making frequent forays over the water from perches on dead snags. A sudden mosquito droned in to light on his cheek and David overreacted by slapping it hard.

"Just you wait," Archie said. "That's the first of billions. We'll have to wear our head nets; in the north men go mad with bugs." He frowned. "As if we didn't have enough troubles."

"We'll get by," David said, but he was worried about Archie's leg, which didn't seem to be healing right. There were times when Archie would sway uncertainly as though blacking out from pain, and the leg still looked purple and angry, not like an injury about to heal.

But even in moments of pain Archie tried to be cheerful. "I'm healing fast," he said. "Pretty soon I'll be packing my share of the load around here."

That night David helped Archie arrange a mosquito net about his bed, then fixed one for his own. For a long time he lay quiet, watching the hungry insects fighting against the net. A vague unrest made it hard to sleep, and he slept only fitfully, awakening at every song and flutter of the birds. He heard splashings from the pond, but they did not seem to concern him and finally he slept.

Had he looked out over the neighboring pond, he might have seen the cow moose as she left the thickets. Nervous with tensions of approaching birth, she browsed slowly out from the shore of the pond while behind her on the beach two frustrated wolves sat on their haunches, contemplating the water, but too wise to get caught in it by an animal that even under normal conditions was dangerous and unpredictable.

For some time the cow browsed, head submerged while she dined on water weeds, raising it only to glance about for danger with small, piglike eyes. She seemed to ignore the trailing wolves, but it was only when they trotted off into the forest that she moved to a small brushy island on the pond.

At another time she would have paid no attention to the gray jays watching her from the spruces. Now she blew at them angrily, rushed forward in a short charge, and pawed at them with slashing hooves until they flew laughing off toward shore. For nearly an hour she stood hidden and watchful for danger, then, as birth pangs wracked her with increasing regularity, tail flicking nervously as though batting at hovering insects, she nosed about for a proper bed, turned round and round, folded her long legs beneath her with a grunt, and lay still.

As her sides began to heave and her breath came in

short gasps, she stretched flat, and soon, from beneath her tail, a pale, bluish, membranous sack appeared, so translucent as to expose the nose and tiny forefeet of her calf. Now and again the harried animal rose to her feet, turned to sniff the ground for a baby, then lay to resume her labors.

As she strained, her nostrils blew steam in great, fevered snorts, and when there seemed to be no more strength in her, she rested, as though asleep, building for another try.

At last, heaving mightily, she strained out head, forelegs, shoulders, then with a rush of wastes and pearly fluid her baby slid out over the ground. Instantly the cow struggled to her feet, breaking the long red umbilical life line, which had fed the developing embryo from her own body. For a moment she butted the fawn as though confused, uncertain whether to love it or batter it down and trample its tiny body into the wet moss. For the moment hatred and love seemed mixed. Then an instinct to mother and protect rose to dominate all else, and she began licking the calf dry with the roughness of her tongue.

Fragile but determined, the calf soon attempted to stand on its big-jointed legs. Time and again it went sprawling. Trembling, it lay in a patch of sunlight, resting, drying out, and coughing to expel remnants of fluid from its lungs. Then, at last, it staggered to its feet, wobbled uncertainly, and made a few faltering steps.

Used to a world of darkness, it seemed almost blind, chewing at bushes and finally at the knobby bones of the cow's hocks. With her huge Roman nose the moose reached backward and rooted the calf, trembling and confused, into position to suck. Instinct lifted its velvety nose upward, along the curve of her hind leg to the softness of her underbelly and the distended udder. Frantically it began to chew until suddenly it found the walnut-sized teat. Then its tail began to flick as the first hot, sugary milk coursed down its throat.

As though sensing a feast, the gray jays returned to the island to search for tidbits. Experience had taught them, perhaps, to associate the rages of a cow moose with the birthing process, and with that blessed event the likelihood of food. At the sight of the new calf the jays called harshly, passing word through the forest, and soon others came winging until there were more than a dozen. As from some age-old instinct to clean up carefully lest predators be attracted to the scene, the moose chewed at the red flag of the sack, which had once housed the calf, while the jays watched hungrily, ready to dart down for any available scrap.

Whenever they grew too bold, the cow blew at them, butted small spruces, and struck into thin air with iron hooves, but the gray demons only laughed harshly at her and retreated out of reach. Today the whole world was her enemy; even the wolves would seek easier prey.

For several hours the following morning the pair lay quietly. Archie and David, a quarter mile away, had no knowledge of their presence.

STRANGE COMPANION

That afternoon, as David strung his bow and prepared to go off to check his snares, Archie struggled to his feet and took up his crude crutches.

"About time I made myself a moving target for these damn bugs and made them work for their grub, at least," Archie said. "I'm tired of cozying up to a smudge fire. Today, I'm going to take Rusty for a walk along the lake."

The boy looked worried. "Better rest under your net and take care of that leg," he warned.

Archie shook his head stubbornly. "A change of scene will do me good."

As the boy moved off into the forest and was lost to sight, the pilot called the crane and together they passed down the trail David had worn through moss and brush to the shore of the pond. Every few feet Archie rested while the young crane, now nearly sixteen inches tall, ran a few feet ahead and looked back quizzically as though wondering why this man was so much slower than David. Rusty piped to him eagerly to urge him on, flapped his short wings, and gave a short hop.

In the thicket on the small island nearby, the huge cow moose raised her head from licking her dozing calf and stared, eyes crackling with anger as Archie hobbled nearer, every successive planting of his crutches swinging him closer to the territory she was determined to defend.

Exploding into action, the cow, in three giant strides, hit the shallows, skidded to a stop, and stood, staring first at the man, then at the crane. She blew a warning, intended to bluff her enemies away.

Across the water Rusty saw the motion and stopped. Perhaps he mistook the figure across the strait for David. With a delighted "Preep!" he waded toward the cow.

Archie saw the moose and the tiny calf wobbling along the shore of the island and knew their danger.

"Rusty!" he called. "Come back, Rusty!"

At the sound of his voice the cow made a short rush, splattering water, then stopped, head shaking in rage, nostrils distended, and black eyes sparkling hatred; she was ready to die in defense of her calf.

To the little whooping crane the splash of water must have sounded like David and fun. As the water deepened, Rusty stood still for a moment, waves lapping at his breast, then once more began to wade.

"Rusty!" Archie pleaded. He felt useless and vulnerable. Damn the leg! "Rusty!" he called again, but now the crane was in water too deep to wade and was paddling frantically. The cow moose was tense, bristling. The man had but one choice. Throwing himself forward on his crutches, he plunged through the shallows to save the bird.

Three-quarters of a ton of cow moose hurtled forward like an express train and plowed a furrow of foaming water as she charged across the shallows toward man and bird. In a desperate attempt to help Rusty Archie hurled his crutches at the moose. The crutches rattled against her shoulders as the moose came on. In an instant the pilot fell beneath her trampling hooves and lay like a sodden scarecrow in the murky waters of the pond.

Washed ashore by her wake, Rusty struggled to his feet and ran blindly toward the thickets. For a moment the cow moose stood bewildered, trembling in her rage, searching for an enemy, but all was quiet. From the island, defying its mother's teachings, the confused and lonely calf bleated plaintively. The cow made a short rush toward the point where Rusty had disappeared, then, as though fearing that her calf's frightened cries would summon a host of wolves, she turned and waded back to its side. Soon, with calf pressed hard against her heaving ribs, she splashed through the pond on the far side of the island and was instantly swallowed by the gloom of the forest.

Nine

AS David trudged into the deserted camp, packing a brace of hares he had snared, he sensed immediately that something was wrong when he saw a host of gray jays raiding the smokehouse. Dropping his load, he rushed forward, scattering the bandits into the surrounding trees, where they filled the forest with their harsh laughter. The fire under the meat, which had kept them away, had gone out, and the birds had flown in and out at will through cracks in the siding, packing away precious strips of jerky to hide in secret places in the forest.

"Archie! Rusty!" he shouted in a sudden panic. Any second now he expected Archie to bellow a reply and Rusty to pipe loudly as he ran to meet him, flapping his growing wings. But there was only silence.

David rushed to the hut in the wrecked fuselage, thinking that perhaps Archie had taken refuge there to escape the growing numbers of mosquitoes and had fallen asleep, but the shelter was empty.

"Archie!" he shouted again. "Archie! Quit playing games and answer me!"

Hurriedly he rekindled the fire under what meat was left in the smokehouse, then followed the deep indentations left by Archie's crutches as the heavy man had swung his way toward the pond. Through brush and sphagnum moss the tracks stayed carefully on the path to the pond, where they turned left and followed the shore. Now and again he came to clusters of indentations, big and small, where Archie had rested for a time and Rusty had probed the soft mud at his feet. Soon the rest stops came at shorter intervals. David read in this that the injured man was beginning to tire and guessed, hopefully, that he would not try to go far.

"Archie!" he shouted again. A male bufflehead, flashing black on white, pattered from the reeds, circled the pond on whistling wings, and splashed down toward the center of the pond. The water vegetation had so grown since his adventure a few short weeks before to gather the egg that it all but obscured the whooping crane nest site, but as the breezes parted the nodding, swaying water grasses, he caught a flash of white and knew that the body of the dead crane was still with the nest.

Mysteriously, Archie's tracks ended abruptly along the shore of the pond, as though a giant eagle had picked the man up and carried him away. Perhaps he had waded into the water, but surely, David reasoned, with his broken leg Archie wouldn't have dared. David made a brief foray into the brush, but the ground was so littered with downed trees, fallen like jackstraws, that even a healthy man could scarcely have gotten through. And where Archie went, he had to leave tracks, pockmarks in the floor of the forest. Here in the trees he could find no sign.

As David returned to the pond, his glance caught the shine of sunlight on what suddenly materialized as two drifting crutches, and he saw that the floating log he had merely glanced at as it drifted among the water vegetation was not a log at all but the body of the pilot floating face downward. "Archie!" David screamed and plunged into the water.

Grasping him by the sleeve, he towed him toward shore. The reeds caught at the body, and as the water became more shallow, Archie became heavier and David could hardly drag him. "Come on, Archie, help me," he sobbed, realizing as he said it that he was being foolish, that Archie was dead and there was no hope. Only when he had rolled and dragged the body onto a patch of dry sand did he pause for breath.

He glanced around him in bewilderment, trying to read the signs. Why had Archie gone into the water? Why were his clothes torn and disheveled as though he had been mauled? A bear might have done it, but there were no claw marks, only bruises. Then, suddenly, he saw the tracks where a moose had come splashing ashore, skidded about, scattering dirt, and charged back into the water again. The fresh tracks were only now crumbling with the assault of waves beginning to rise with the wind against the shore.

The moose could have been a cow with a new calf hidden somewhere in the brush. Kise had warned him to stay away from wild animals with young; they hated the world.

Little by little David pieced together what had happened. Too stunned now to weep, he stood helplessly looking down at the man. Archie's leg jutted at an odd angle from its brace, and David realized that Archie must have been keeping from him the fact that the leg had never really knit. Swiftly and painlessly the moose had done for Archie what the broken leg would surely have done in time, but only after an agony of suffering.

Now he was totally alone. Even Rusty was gone, trampled perhaps into the bottom muck of the pond or eaten by a predator as the poor frightened crane rushed up and down the beach piping frantically, waiting for Archie to rise from the marsh. For a long time David sat beside Archie's body, utterly defeated, letting the tears run at will down his cheeks.

It was the mosquitoes that finally drove him into action. During the heat of the day they had stayed hidden in the mosses and shade of the forest. Now as a few scattered clouds passed over the sun and a chill swept over the land, the mosquitoes, came out in force to torment the boy. Rising to his feet as he swung at them madly, David took his head net from his pocket and tied it firmly in place.

Working quickly, he scraped some heavy sphagnum moss into a huge pile, then mustering all his strength, he dragged Archie into the shallow grave. From his friend's pocket, he took his treasured pocketknife and waterproof container of matches, then quietly and more in control, covered the body carefully with moss and logs. When he had constructed a large mound over the body, he picked golden dandelions and laid a wreath of them on the grave. From the top of a tamarack a white-throated sparrow sang once and was silent. Save for lap of wave and hum of insects there was no sound.

For a time David waded through the reeds, looking for some sign of the young crane, but found not even a feather. Moving off into the woods, he roamed the glades near the pond, calling to the lost bird in hopes that Rusty had hidden somewhere in his fright. Sometimes a fox yapped back in answer, but there was no sign of the bird. He took each path near the camp where Rusty had followed him before, half expecting to see him ahead as he moved around each bend, to hear his voice answering from each brushy thicket. On and on he went even though he realized that his chances of finding the little whooping crane were growing more and more remote.

It was only when exhaustion drove him back to

camp that he gave up the search. He ate a piece of dried meat, then threw himself down on his bed. The tears began to flow again, gushes of grief, homesickness, loneliness, and fear all mingled together. He wanted to be back in his bed in the old farmhouse near Edmonton, listening to the wind in the eaves and hearing Kise's murmured voice drifting up the stairwell as he sat playing cribbage with his friend Elmore Claridge, the milkman. He tried to think of all manner of things, but his mind kept flashing back to the sight of Archie lying in the water and Archie lying in his shallow grave atop the permafrost. He kept seeing Rusty—Rusty being devoured by a fox, a wolf, a goshawk, Rusty being trampled by an enraged cow moose. The campfire collapsed upon its embers and he slept.

"Preep!" The voice came to him as though out of his past, out of a dream. "Preep!" Rusty's voice haunting him, pestering him out of his sleep, coming perhaps out of the belly of a fox. Closer now. Suddenly, more than a voice, a small crane beak nibbling at his ear and soft down against his chapped cheeks. Astonished, David raised himself on his elbow and stared. There beside him, bedraggled but alive, stood the little whooping crane begging to be fed.

"Rusty!" David caught up the startled bird and held him tight to his chest. He rushed to the pond, seized a handful of snails from a submerged log, crushed them in his hand, and offered them to the bird, who wolfed them down and demanded more. Whatever ordeals the young crane had been through seemed suddenly forgotten in the rush to fill his stomach.

The loss of Archie was easier to bear now that he had found Rusty. No longer did he feel alone.

Returning to camp with Rusty trailing close at his heels, he built a roaring fire, and as the smoke towered above the surrounding forests, he felt that somehow it must be visible to all the world, somehow it must make contact with others of his kind. Perhaps with an Indian canoeing up a river or even a prospector looking for minerals. He could not believe that with patience and continued effort to survive he would not be found.

Archie's wrist watch had seemed a link to civilization, and the pilot had guarded it zealously, keeping it carefully wound lest he lose track of time. But the watch had drowned with him. Now without a clock, and without a barrier of darkness to separate one day from the next, each blended with the morrow.

As the weather became hotter, more and more mosquitoes hatched in the marshes and went hunting in a howling pack until David and Rusty were forced to seek shelter in the fuselage, where he plugged the cracks with sphagnum moss and kept a smudge of green spruce boughs smoldering to keep the insects out. During the heat of the day, while the sun drove the insects to shade and made an inferno of the metal shelter, David worked at laying in his food supply.

The arctic hares remained a staple in his diet, with an occasional grouse to vary the monotony, and greens were prevalent. He skimmed quantities of lemna, or duckweed, from the ponds for salad and boiled young, tender nettles into spinach. What food he could not eat, he dried and hung in the tin hut.

Now and again he would touch off a big bonfire near the camp, hoping that the smoke would attract a passing plane. Beyond that there was little he could do to effect his rescue except hope, and try to keep up his strength.

As June slipped somehow into July, there were many changes in the young whooping crane: he skyrocketed in height, rust-colored feathers covered the down, cuteness gave way to awkward adolescence, and his beak hardened into steel. He had no conscience about hammering a kneecap until David yelped in pain, pulling off blankets as David tried to sleep, snatching away his mosquito netting, or tweaking his ears as though he intended to tear them up and devour them.

Sometimes when his trap line failed to yield much, David was forced to put up with the insects and go farther afield for food. On even the hottest days he wore his jacket, covering his head carefully with his head net to keep the swarming clouds out of nose, mouth, eyes, and ears. In all the land insects seemed in control. Moose and wood bisons made wallows in the marshes, coating themselves with muddy armor or submerging until only heads and horns showed above water. Because of their heavy coats, wolves fared better, though sometimes David saw them snap angrily at tormenting flies and paw them off ears and eyelids.

Gnats, or no-see-ums, crawled up his sleeves and cuffs, making his forearms and shins burn, but the hardest to bear were the black flies, which bit

through the eyelets of his boots to draw blood, leaving a torment of an itch where it was hardest to scratch.

Without Archie as a baby sitter, David could no longer leave Rusty in camp. Thus, much as he hindered progress, David took him along, waiting patiently as the crane satisfied his curiosity by hammering away with his beak at everything of interest along the way.

Protected by the boy from predators, stuffed with handouts augmented by what he could glean from the wild, the crane at this point had a far greater chance of survival than his wild brethren. He was the center now of David's life, and each new feather a point of interest. Somehow, David had expected Rusty's plumage to be snowy white like that of his parents, but instead he wore a coat stained with rust, his eyes were brown instead of yellow, and his head was totally feathered, without the bare crimson skin of adulthood.

As he grew, so did his energies, and when he was not feeding or trailing David, he was working the soil with his restless beak as though fighting a perpetual itch, which could be scratched only by endless probing in the ground.

Patiently David helped him across barricades of windfalls and walked slowly when the going was tough, so Rusty could keep up. He was no help at all on the hunt. Often when David had used his art to set a snare with utmost delicacy, Rusty would seize the wire with his beak, ruining the set, and David would have to start all over again.

Eternally curious, Rusty often ignored his mentor

to explore the world, happily busy until that point when the boy disappeared from sight in a thicket. Forgetting his exploration, the crane would charge ahead, piping frantically, wings spread, hunting David on the run. He would frighten away any game David might be stalking, sending grouse thundering out of the thickets and hares thumping along their runs.

But the bird was not insensitive to the boy's moods. Often the immensity of the land, homesickness, and the stark reality of their plight would combine to get David down. He would sit on a log, seeking an exposed place in the sun, where insects were less fierce, and the salt tears would rush in a flood, soaking his head net. Then Rusty, sensing his depression, would amble over, and shedding his usual indifference, cock his head and look up at the boy's face. He would nibble gently at his trousers or the laces of his boots, piping softly some whooping crane endearment, whose meaning the boy could only guess.

Even more spectacular than the development of the crane was the change in David himself. He was a bit taller and thinner, his clothes were more tattered, and his hair was long and unruly, but the real change was in his character and independence. For a time he had clung to the familiar scenes around the camp as though he still needed comfort from memories or even the nearness of Archie's grave, but now he realized that the signal fires and the SOS had not worked, that hope was dimming with each passing day, and that he would have to save himself by trying to reach civilization.

Now that Rusty was able to travel, he saw that his best chance lay in striking off on a straight course across the country. His journey might be three hundred miles or five hundred, and he must start soon, for July was almost gone and there was not all that much time before winter. In order to keep from wandering in circles, he would have to blaze trees and forge a straight line by sighting ahead and backward along their trail.

Once more he looked at the map, studying the point Archie had marked as being their most probable position. The best chance, Archie had said, was to try to hit the road running from Fort Smith to Hay River on Great Slave Lake. Almost every day, Archie claimed, supply trucks passed by, delivering fuel and supplies to distribution points in the north. David saw himself emerging from the brush after a long trek, tattered and dirty, hair shoulder length, flagging down a truck and showing a doubting driver the distance he had traveled on the map from the point where the plane had gone down hundreds of miles away.

His first problem was to establish directions. The trick was to remember on what side of the neighboring thicket snow had lain the longest in the spring and to decide which side of the trees had the heaviest shadows. An error of a few degrees might cause him to miss the road and send him off into hundreds of miles of desolation.

By now he had a good supply of dried food, but

to blaze a trail he needed an axe. Scavenging a piece of steel from the wreckage, David built a fire of pitchy spruce, made a crude set of bellows from sheet metal, and fanned the blaze into a roaring heat. Just as he'd seen Kise do on the old blacksmith forge on the farm, he heated the steel cherry-red. He was glad now that he'd helped so many times, cranking the bellows for the old man as he made horseshoes or even parts for broken hay machinery. Now, using one big rock as an anvil and another as a primitive hammer, David beat the glowing iron into the shape of a crude axe, complete with handle, then tempered it hard by immersing it, hissing and bubbling, into the pond.

When the axe had cooled, David hefted it and felt elated. Kise would have been proud of him; it was a pretty good tool at that! While the fire was still hot, David reheated the handle and punched a hole for a cord by driving a short bolt from the fuselage through the hot metal into soft wood. It was not so neat as a drilled hole, but it was adequate. When he had retempered the handle, he inserted a piece of rope, then hung the axe over his shoulder. Now as he traveled, his hands would be free to hold his bow and arrows in readiness in case he saw game.

Once the axe was finished, he busied himself converting Archie's duffel into a backpack, which he filled with those items from the camp that he could best use for survival.

The decision to strike out over the land came as a relief, and once he had made up his mind, he did not change it. He was not worried about Rusty.

While the bird would slow him down, he would stick with him just as he had on excursions past. But for the present the crane was worse than useless, for he took the loading of the pack to be a game, and as fast as David stowed items in, Rusty dragged them out with his probing beak and scattered them until David finally distracted the bird by tossing a meal of fresh snails on the ground.

The ruse worked for a few moments only. Rusty was adept at spearing a dragonfly off a stalk or finding his own snails, but he still preferred the attention involved in having David feed him from his fingers. Thus he was soon back underfoot. He seemed to sense that something different was going on; perhaps the excitement David felt over the journey was mirrored in the young crane. Soon he began to run back and forth about the camp, flexing his growing wings as though conditioning them for travel.

Then all was done. David was ready, and there were no more excuses to stay. He double-checked his pack. In it were snares, the map, matches, extra clothes, Archie's heavy jacket, and as much dried food as he could carry. He shouldered the heavy burden, took his axe and bow and arrows, called Rusty, and without so much as a backward glance at the grave or the camp that had been his home, headed north, trying to hit the Fort Smith-Hay River highway, leaving the wreckage to the jays and insects.

From the trees the jays watched him go, jabbering merrily. His head rang with echoes. He felt Archie's presence and seemed to hear his laughter from beyond the grave. "You need any help along the way, you just phone me, Davey boy. OK? And if you see the President, tell him I'm sorry I put a dent in his airplane!"

Striding on, careful lest his head net, so vital to his existence, catch and tear on the brush, he blazed a tree on opposite sides, north and south, lined ahead to another and blazed it, and used the first two to sight ahead to a third, surveying a straight line due north. The blazes gave him a feeling of security, for he knew he could always follow them back to camp. The moving was slow and difficult, but he kept traveling as fast as he felt Rusty could follow. Soon he had left his hunting ranges behind and was in unfamiliar territory. Each step in the damp knee-deep moss took its toll of his strength, the straps from the pack cut his shoulders painfully, and every bite of an insect tapped not only his blood supply but the reservoir of his patience.

He had gone perhaps three miles when he was forced to rest in the middle of a large clearing, stretching out on the soft moss in full sunshine so that the shade-loving insects would give him respite.

He was tired, but somehow his spirits were buoyed by a resolve to enjoy his desperate gamble as an adventure. Somewhere from afar a hermit thrush sang a song familiar since his childhood, and in the thin, silvery sweetness of that melancholy hymn he found solace and reassurance. With Rusty cuddled against him, he slept.

Ten

TO splash across a land two-thirds water was an ordeal David wouldn't have wished on a water spaniel. Much as he feared the mysterious boggy sloughs and dark aimless rivers winding indeterminably through brushy thickets of stunted willow, dwarf birch, black spruce, and tamarack, he had no choice but to plow through, for to go around a pond was to risk putting a small, but perhaps critical bend in the straight line he was attempting to draw to the north.

At their approach, across the ponds broods of still-flightless ducklings skittered into the grasses and were lost to view while the parents engaged in frantic broken-wing acts to lead the interlopers away.

With unquestioning faith the tall, awkward rust-colored young whooping crane followed David into the water, wading the shallows, but where the water became too deep, he propelled himself along by flapping his wings like some huge flightless flopping duck. At times beaver dams made handy bridges for David. Rather than brave the treachery of sticks stuck helter-skelter into mud, or swim the deep water above the dam, Rusty preferred to wade the shallows immediately below the structure, where not only did he find a better crossing, but enjoyed the chance of spearing a tadpole or two.

That evening as the two companions trudged wearily across a mile or so of perceptibly higher ground, David caught the shine of water ahead through the trees. Breaking out of the thickets, he found himself on the edge of a dark, mysterious lake. The shoreline was thronged with stunted spruces that tossed in the breeze like the manes of rearing horses.

While David set up camp on a spit of land jutting into the lake, where the insects seemed at a minimum, then wandered off to set a few snares in adjoining thickets, Rusty waded out into the shallows, drank, bathed noisily, then patrolled the reeds, hunting frogs, dragonfly larvae, and snails. Frequently he looked up from his probing to reassure himself that his friend was near.

STRANGE COMPANION

David was in the midst of setting a snare when Rusty called in distress. Out beyond the startled crane David could see what at first appeared to be a partially submerged log, drifting through clusters of pondweeds. It was obvious from the wake that the log was moving their way in no uncertain fashion. For a moment Rusty stared fearfully, then took off, splashing through the shallows at a long-legged lope toward David.

For a time the log was still, until David felt that he had only imagined what he had seen. Then, suddenly, it began moving directly toward them. David was ready to seize Rusty and flee when the monster burst from its wake. It was only a bull moose, looking ridiculous with antlers in velvet, dripping gushes of pond water as he raised his head from feeding along the bottom. From the bull's mouth trailed a garland of water weeds, which he munched quietly as he glanced their way, then submerged for more.

Once David had dined on hare and dandelion greens, he took off his wet clothes, climbed into Archie's old flight suit, and tried to drive away his half-drowned feeling by drinking scalding tea, made by boiling young tips of birch, shrubby cinquefoil, and a plant Kise had shown him, Labrador tea. It tasted flat, like the last cup of tea from a much-used tea bag, and needed sugar, but it was better than plain boiled water from the sloughs, and picked up his spirits.

As David lay quiet, resting his aching muscles, he

watched as a beaver swam his nearsighted way along the shore, pushing before him a length of aspen log, bound to dine at some favorite spot or to anchor it deep in mud near his lodge for winter use. Eyeing the intruders on shore, he drifted for a moment, slapped his tail in alarm, dove, then resurfaced to drift again. At length, the beaver took his log, and nosing it like a tugboat pushing a freighter, moved it up the lake.

The wind had died, and across the glassy calm, a black bear with twin cubs ambled along the beach. Obligingly the mother turned over logs or rocks while the cubs licked away any insects she exposed. Now and again the sow bear stood on her hind legs to peer across the deep at the campfire, but the expanse of water made both bear and boy feel safer, and soon the bear family, after a noisy romp in the shallows, moved, dripping, back into the forests.

Behind David, somewhere back along their trail, a timber wolf howled, breaking the silence of the whelping season, and soon was answered by another across the lake. Others joined from afar until the whole forest echoed with their calls. The voices had to have a meaning, and David hoped they weren't discussing him.

In the distance he heard a hermit thrush—perhaps the selfsame one—silver voiced, thanking the heavens for its solitude. From the trees along the shore white-throated sparrows sang incessantly, and with this lullaby in his ears, David drifted off to sleep as Rusty stood on one leg in the nearby shallows, taking catnaps but alert to danger.

Early the next morning as he struggled to awake from a refreshing sleep, David dreamed that he was being attacked by a giant mosquito, but sat bolt upright to find it was only Rusty hammering hard at his shin. Obviously distressed, the bird needed the reassurance of David's company. Suddenly the boy knew why. Echoing from the forests ringing the lake came weird, demonic laughter. His heart pounded hard, and he grabbed his boots, ready to flee. On the lake there was nothing but the mists of early morning, chasing about like silvery ghosts before vanishing above the watching circle of trees.

David shivered. "Hsst! Rusty!" he whispered. "Let's scram out of here!" As though he understood, the crane cocked his head and listened. Again came the sound, wild, mysterious, as from some madwoman lost upon the other shore.

Hardly daring to risk attracting attention by moving, David took a sneak look about camp, locating his bow, his axe, and his pack.

The sound came closer. David listened hard, a cold sweat breaking out over him. He crouched ready to spring and run, then suddenly he relaxed and dissolved in laughter, hugging the startled crane. "Well, we're a pair of fools! It's a loon, of course!" Closer came the laughter and suddenly David saw the bird swimming just offshore, looking all head and neck as it swam with body submerged. As David stood up, the loon dove like a flash, and when it surfaced again, it was a quarter of a mile away.

Checking his snare line, David found a hare, but not being hungry, he dressed it out and put it away in his pack for his evening meal. Marking a point across the lake in line with his travels, he gathered his possessions, called Rusty to his side, and skirted along the brushy shoreline until he had gained the landmark. Then, sighting back at the point where they had spent the night, he moved off into the forest, and within a few hundred yards, the lake was lost to view.

Bear tracks were everywhere, the tracks of the cubs resembling those of a barefoot child. He was relieved when he left their territory without meeting the mother bear face-to-face in the thickets. Archie's death had taught him that animals with young need to be given wide berth.

Often, as day followed day, to keep track of passing time, David tried to recall the different camps, but other than the spit of land at Loon Lake, one blurred with another. His marches lacked urgency, and drugged at night with fatigue, he slept through the noises of the land and awoke not really sure if he had slept twelve hours or twenty-four. He knew that winter was the deadline when he must complete his journey, but with the hot summer sun beating down, turning the mosses beneath his feet to dust, that time seemed far away.

Now and again as he sat resting—watching Rusty feed among reeds and grasses of a bog, catch damselflies, butterflies, and moths, or probe in the mud for worms—he thought dreamily of Kise and the farm and wondered if anyone knew by now that he had been a passenger on that ill-fated plane or if they had looked for him in the cities where runaways usually go. The outside world now had the quality of a dream, and sometimes he was not really sure that it existed or, if it existed, if he really cared to reach it.

So tired. So very, very tired. He wished Kise were here, if there had ever really been a Kise. He was tired of making decisions for himself, tired of blazing trees, of sighting ahead to determine where to go, of planning what to eat and where to stop, of watching constantly for danger on their trail, of being responsible for Rusty, one of the last of a vanishing species. Every time he ate a new plant, he risked getting ill; Kise would know for sure which of the northern plants were good to eat and which were poisonous. So far he had been lucky.

If he had run away partly because Kise had pushed him too hard, demanded too much, now he felt the old man's presence through what Kise had taught him to do. What other boy his age would know to gather stinging nettles, boil away the irritating hairs, and turn the mess into a delicious spinach? What other boy would know to make a salad of the new fronds of ferns, soup of rock tripe, a kind of lichen, or to eat the contents of a grouse's crop or an animal's intestine for vitamins to keep one from getting sick from scurvy, a fatal sickness caused by eating only meat? According to Kise, the natives of

the north stayed healthy on meat diets because, unlike the white men, who loved steaks, they relished the intestines and their contents and thus gained a source of vitamins the white man usually got from vegetables.

It was mid-July when David and Rusty emerged at the edge of a large marsh to see in the distance a pair of whooping cranes with one young bird feeding beside them.

David puffed with parental pride. "Look at that, Rusty! You're much bigger and more beautiful than that young one, which proves that I'm a better parent than the wild cranes."

The whooping cranes sighted the intruders and bugled loudly. "Kerloo! Kerloo!" At the sound the youngster vanished into the vegetation. Rusty seemed frightened by the commotion and moved closer to David for safety. The boy could have spent hours watching the rare sight, but he felt like an intruder, and so the strange companions, boy and crane, moved on, leaving the marsh behind.

Bugling loudly, the great white male flew over them to determine their whereabouts, and once again David thrilled to see that snowy breast, the glow of light through seven-foot wings and fan-shaped tail, the glorious crimson of the facial markings, the black moustache, and the great yellow eyes.

Content that they were leaving his territory behind and meant no harm to his chick, the crane turned slow, easy circles, with only occasional wing beats for elevation. Then in a long effortless glide he swept across forest and marsh to rejoin his family. In the distance David heard his swaggering call of triumph, claiming victory over intruders from the field. David tipped back his head and tried to come up with his own mocking challenge, but his voice lacked the buglelike resonance of the crane's twenty-four-foot trachea and was muted almost immediately by the mosses and the forest. Rusty seemed to ignore his effort, and together the two friends moved on into the unknown land.

Eleven

BY August Rusty had left all remnants of his baby fuzz hanging from the brush along the trail, and wore a trim, handsome suit of rust-brown feathers enlivened with white. His wing and pinion feathers were sprouting fast, and the quills were blue-black, heavy with blood. Most of his waking moments, when not traveling, he spent preening the flaking itch from each feather with his saberlike beak. Soon, David realized with some misgivings, the five-foot-tall crane would be able to take to the air and sail over the land, leaving him grounded.

The northern summer is all too short. More than in southern lands one senses an impatience among all wildlife to reproduce and raise their young before ice covers the land and living is hazardous.

Courtship is often loud, frantic, and unsubtle, with little time for errors or renestings. Due to the long hours of daylight, the search for food and feeding of the young is an almost constant affair, so that the young grow quickly and are soon tumbling from burrow or nest.

David was impressed all too suddenly with a sense of summer's passing. Where once he had found nests of juncos and white-crowned sparrows hidden beneath fallen logs, and the young, feeling the ground tremble at his approach, had gaped their yellow mouths at him to be fed, now the nests were empty and the young had flown.

In the marshes Rusty had hated the blackbirds with a passion. Fearlessly protective of their young, they had ridden perched upon his back or fluttered down to peck at his head. He had tried his best to rub them off or to stab them with his beak, but without success; as he left the territory of one pair and had a moment's relief, he moved into that of another, and the scolding nuisance began again. But now in August the young blackbirds, flushing in waves before them from the bending reeds, resembled their molting parents, and the adults no longer challenged their passing. Buffleheads, widgeons, scaups, and redheads sailed their broods in fleets upon the ponds, the young no longer skittering across the water peeping frantically when left behind.

STRANGE COMPANION

As the summer progressed, the nights became dark once more. David welcomed the change. Not only was it easier to rest, but the hares increased their activity and were more easily snared. As he traveled, he tried to provide the needs of the day, saving his supply of dried meat for some vague, not-to-be-thought-about emergency in the future.

Often he thought he detected a subtle change in the terrain and hoped for higher, firmer ground, but the next day he would find himself back in rough going, fighting knee-deep moss, wet clothing, swamps, rivers, and thickets, which seemed to leap before him to confuse his way. There was a chill to the early mornings, and he tried to end each day by drying out his clothing by a campfire.

One day in late August, as he skirted the shore of a large beaver dam, he noticed schools of fish sunning themselves in the shallows, ever retreating to deeper water as he approached. He had hoped to find trout or grayling in these waters, but the long, thin snouts of the fish showed them to be northern pike. Pike are a rank, inferior species—slimy, foul odored, and hard to skin—but his mouth watered, for any change of diet would be welcome.

Leaving Rusty to probe for food in the marshy ooze along shore, David picked his way over the sharp sticks of the dam to where the water was deepest. Not far from where he stood, a huge beaver house of mud and branches formed an island in the pond. Freshly gnawed aspen and willow sticks were scattered fresh and white among the weathered gray sticks of the dome, showing recent activity. Staring down into the coffee-colored murk, he saw huge drifting shadows, which could only have been giant pike of a size he had never before seen.

In his pack he had brought along a fishing line of fine wire, robbed from the plane's electrical circuits for just such an event. It was a precious item in his survival kit; he had hoarded it against the possibility he would one day have to fish through the ice to survive.

He had no hooks, but he remembered back to a trip along the Athabaska with Kise when their canoe had shipped water and capsized in the rapids and Kise had lost his fishing tackle box in the deeps. Kise hadn't even gotten angry, but had shown him how to fish without hooks, and that evening in a tributary they had caught a meal of fat trout.

Now David cut a willow stick some two inches long, notched it in the middle, and attached the line. Then he impaled a chunk of fresh meat with the wood so that when a fish swallowed the bait, tension on the line would turn the stick crosswise in its stomach.

He was about to cut his precious line in two sections for safekeeping, when a huge splash just off shore excited him so much he threw out his bait into the deep water beside the dying swirl. Instantly a giant pike bolted from the depths, smashed at the bait, and swallowed it whole. "Hey, Rusty!" he called. "Look over here. I've got a monster on!"

He gave the fish plenty of time to get the bait down into his stomach, hardly daring to breathe as the line payed out slowly and evenly as the fish sank into deeper water. "Now!" David cried and gave a quick jerk to turn the stick. The line jerked tight as though he had snagged a giant log, then swiftly the water boiled and the line hissed through his fingers, cutting his flesh like a knife, and he knew too late that he should have used some sort of pole. In his excitement he had failed to think ahead and now he must pay the price. Inch by inch the fish fought out the line to the end. David wrapped it about his wrist and inch by inch fought it back.

The logs of the beaver dam were covered with slime, and he half fell, trying to keep his footing. The huge pike raced close, drenching the boy with spray as it leaped high, but before David could gather the slack, the fish was far away again, making great smacking leaps out in the middle of the pond. Again it charged close and leaped as though trying to have a look at him. Swiftly the fish raced away before David could gather the slack. The line thrummed under tension and David feared it would break and be lost as the giant sought the depths and sulked. David felt the hot blood dripping down his fingers from his cuts, but there was no chance to inspect the damage; his gaze riveted on the spot where the line disappeared into the murk. Slowly he increased the tension on the line and little by little he began to win it back.

Once more the monster crashed to the surface and jumped, but David sensed the fish was beginning to tire. He could just picture the great white-meated fillets dripping their juices into the fire; he could smell their fragrance and taste the sweet, delicious flesh. Gently, confidently, he pulled the huge creature toward him. It seemed passive now, and he thought he could slide it out of the water. He could see the huge gaping mouth slashing the snout, the vicious teeth, and the great stupid buttonlike eyes.

Trembling with excitement and the prospect of food, he knelt to hook his fingers in the gills and drag the monster out of its element.

Frightened by his touch, the pike exploded, drenched David with water, and swirled away. The line hummed through David's fingers as he tried to seize it, blood spurted afresh, and suddenly line and fish were gone and the pond was quiet, as though the episode had never taken place.

It was not the loss of the fish that bothered him most but of the line. Desperately he searched the bottom of his pack for more but found none. He had been stupid. Why hadn't he divided the precious line in two? Why hadn't he fished where the fish were smaller and less apt to take his tackle and run?

For a long time he sat watching the pond, hoping that the fish would somehow foul himself on a snag so that he might recover the line, but apparently all the fish in the pond had retreated to the depths with the disturbance and there was not even a ripple. More discouraged than he had been since Archie's death, he picked his way back across the dam to shore and called Rusty, who had been feeding nonchalantly along the margins of the pond.

He put his arm around the crane. "Know what I am, Rusty? A doggone fool."

That evening, as they rested on a dry knoll, David sat staring into the embers of his campfire and thought about the great pike and the loss of his fish line. He was wiser now. Much as he loved the north and felt at home, he knew that he could not hope to make further mistakes and live.

By late August the moss had become tinder dry from hot winds and long exposure to sunlight. In the air was a bluish haze from distant forest fires, caused perhaps by lightning. Now and again he came to clearings where recent fires had burned unchecked and had finally eaten their way to the edges of ponds, where they died a quick death.

Since he could not skirt the burns without risking a change in his direction, David plunged on through, blazing the charred trunks as he went. Black dust choked his lungs and covered his clothing, but there was no one to see him or laugh at him. Crossing a windfall and blinded by dust, he tore the knee in his pants. Sore as his hands were from his cuts, he managed to pucker the tear together with snare wire.

The insect hordes that had plagued him during the summer were gone now. Emerging from a burn, he found himself on the shore of a small lake. Setting up camp, he took off his clothes and washed them, putting them out on bushes to dry. The chill of autumn was already in the water, but he waded in and bathed, amazed at the dark rivulets of soot that coursed down his chest from his face and hair. He looked down at his body, so long covered by clothes against insects, and was embarrassed by its whiteness once the dirt was gone. But his palms were calloused from the axe, his leg muscles were hard to the touch, and his body was lean, with no trace of the chubbiness of boyhood. For a time he soaked his sore hands in water, then lay in the waning sunshine as his clothes dried. He had perhaps averaged five miles per day, and behind him lay the long line of blazes linking him to the plane and Archie's grave, now some two hundred miles away.

On the next day he emerged from the wetlands into parklands of aspen, mingled with white birch. David hardly dared hope, but when the same scene greeted him the following day, he felt that at long last he was out of the marsh desolations, and travel would be far easier.

On this high ground buffaloes were more numerous and frightening. Huge solitary bulls, whipped by rivals from the herd, pawed dirt over their backs and glared at Rusty and David as though ready to explode into a charge. Larger than the bison of the plains, they attained weights of more than a ton; they existed today only because when the plains buffaloes were being cruelly slaughtered, a small population of these woods bison had managed to survive in this desolate, impenetrable wasteland, where man rarely ventured. Kise had hunted them as a boy, and sometimes in one of his rare talkative moods, before a campfire, he had told David of them until the boy could almost imagine how they looked, sounded, and smelled and could almost taste their meat cooked over a willow fire.

David soon got used to their watchful presence, but their unpredictability kept him edgy. Once as he trailed through a thick aspen forest, he stumbled upon a herd of some two hundred animals lying in the shade. Ahead of him he heard the warning snort of a bull, and suddenly, with crashing of brush and rumbling of hooves, the herd stampeded toward him, each animal adding to the panic of its neighbor.

Between the trees he caught flashes of them milling, bobbing, running blindly and stupidly, with no idea of where danger lay. A century before, Indians had used these tendencies to stampede buffalo herds over cliffs to their death. Seizing the startled crane, David chose the largest aspen he could find and huddled behind it just as a flood of buffaloes engulfed him. Rusty managed a loud squawk of terror and kicked his legs violently to be free, but David held fast, and suddenly the herd was past and gone as quickly as it had come. He dropped Rusty and sagged to the ground, heart thumping wildly, choking on the dust that now hung motionless in the aisles between the trees. It was some minutes before he had collected his wits enough to travel.

A week or two into the month of September, and perhaps two months after leaving the plane, David emerged from an aspen forest to see before him a river far wider than any he had passed before. Rusty was thirsty and the sight of the foaming brown torrent excited him. Where he had shown some rudiments

of the whooping crane dance before, now, even without contact with others of his species, the instinct to dance welled within his breast. Picking up a small stick in his beak, Rusty tossed it into the air, then bounded high, flapping his wings and pirouetting in a fair imitation of the dance grown whooping cranes have been doing since the Pleistocene.

At another moment David might have joined Rusty in his spontaneous outburst of joy. But the sight of the river shocked him. Brown and mysterious, it was clearly too deep to wade and too swift and ripped by undertows to swim. Hoping for an easier crossing, he scouted far upstream and downstream, but around every bend the sight was the same, a roaring, merciless torrent, blocking his way to freedom.

"We've got to get to that far bank, Rusty," he said above the roar. "We've just got to." His fingers touched lightly against the back of the bird's head, and the crane turned and nibbled at his fingers, croaking some tender whooping crane endearment.

As he watched the river a battered log floating past was sucked down by mysterious undercurrents, and when it surfaced again was far downstream, almost around the next bend. The sight left David shaken; if he decided to brave the river, he would have to be careful.

That night they camped along the shore. In the thickets David found a covey of grouse, and with an arrow from his bow, shot one of the foolish birds off a spruce branch for his supper. The white meat was succulent, juicy, and sweet, although a pinch of salt would have done wonders for the taste. For a time after finishing his meal, he sat watching the swirling torrent rushing ever onward, and was relieved when darkness finally screened the river from view.

The next morning he awoke to the calling of a loon, and raised from his bed just in time to see Rusty let loose one of his socks into the current. David rushed to the shore but the sock was gone. Flapping his wings as though in satisfaction, Rusty began to hunt another object with which to play.

"Fool bird!" David grumbled. "Can't you ever do anything useful?"

As though in answer, Rusty picked up a broken section of reed and tossed it into the river, where it bobbed for a moment like a cork before it was caught by the currents and began to sail off like a tiny ship downstream. Meanwhile Rusty wandered back up the bank looking for more diversions.

For a moment David watched the buoyant reed, then suddenly an idea came to him. "Rusty! You just might have shown me something." Taking Archie's pocketknife, he cut some reeds along the bank, knotted them into a bundle, and launched them on the torrent. As he had guessed, the inner air cells made the reeds ride high on the water. In his excitement the boy clapped his hands and jumped up and down. "It'll work," he said. "We'll build a raft of reeds and sail across without even wetting a toenail."

Caught up by his excitement, Rusty began his own dance along the shore. He even tried to help David gather reeds at the water's edge, but he made such a mess of David's neat piles as he tossed the reeds with his beak that the boy scolded him firmly but tenderly and placed the bundles out of reach.

For hours the boy labored patiently. His hands hurt him, and his back ached from endless stooping to cut the reeds low near the water line, but still he labored on until he had worked nearly a mile of shoreline and packed the reeds to a central location. Taking his axe, he cut a quantity of willow, from which he peeled long strips of bark; these he soaked in water to make them more pliable, then wove them into rope.

The finished product was not very stout and broke frequently as he tried to tie the reeds in small tight bundles, but little by little he worked away and soon had reduced the huge pile of reeds to enough bulky sheaves to make a raft. Laying these side by side, he used up his remaining supply of rope to tie them together into a craft large enough to float one boy, one pack, and one whooping crane.

Floating the strange craft along the shore, he added a long aspen pole, cut from a thicket, for a rudder, placed his pack securely on his back, and tried to push Rusty aboard.

"Awwk!" Rusty squawked and tried to flee past him.

"All aboard, Rusty," David commanded, pushing the bird onto the ark. Once the bird had accepted his lot and had settled at one end to explore the deck with his beak, David pushed bravely out into the torrent, using the pole as a rudder with which to steer.

The center of the raft sagged under his weight and

a foaming wave of water crashed over the fragile craft, drenching David to the skin. Rusty flapped his wings delightedly as though the adventure were one more game. As the bubbles of foam washed over the deck, Rusty seized at them with his beak, croaking with delight as they popped and vanished. He flapped his wings and leaped high, almost missing the craft as he came down.

As the contraption bobbed like a cork upon the torrent, David felt a surge of pride. Already they had gained the middle of the river, and there was no apparent reason why the rest of the voyage would not be just as successful. The raging current was carrying them downstream at a fearful rate, but with the aid of his pole, little by little David was steering them toward the far shore.

So busy was he with his navigation chores that he failed to notice that Rusty had begun to worry the crude knots in the fragile willow ropes with his strong beak, and of all the knots to pick he had chosen a vital one in the rope that held the front end of the craft together.

"Rusty!" David shouted above the roar of the water. "Cut that out!" The boy dropped his pole just as the knot came loose. He had time only to check for his pack as the craft disintegrated and they were swept away by the churning river.

David's first thought was for his friend, but he need not have worried, for Rusty, buoyed up by the hollow feathers and bones of his body, had immediately surfaced and was bobbing merrily down the stream like

a great brown swan. "Preep!" he called excitedly as though to say to David, "Hey, look at me!"

The boy felt the flat of his axe slam against his thigh as the current whirled it like a trolling spinner, then suddenly the cord loosened and the tool so important to his welfare was gone. He sputtered, blew water, sank, bounced along the gravel bottom, shot up to the surface, gasped for breath, made a stroke for shore, then promptly sank again as the undertow caught him and twisted him into the shape of a pretzel. Weighted by heavy boots, his legs swung like pendulums, holding him down. Flailing about, he closed his fingers upon a bundle of reeds and clung desperately as the swirl of water almost wrenched it from his grasp. He clutched the bundle hard to his chest, knowing that in the buoyancy of the reeds lay his only chance. Sucking air into his burning lungs, he kicked hard for shore.

The current spun him around and seemed determined to fling him back toward the churning millrace in midstream, but still he hung on. A water-logged stump, eroded from a bank somewhere far upstream, struck him a heavy blow between his shoulders just above his pack, and the roots felt like the tentacles of some giant octopus encircling his neck and tangling in his hair. He screamed in terror and wrenched away from its grasp.

Then, suddenly, one knee dragged bottom, and he straightened both legs, fighting cramps and kicking hard against the bottom rocks toward shore. The swirling current forced him outward again, sucking his feet out from under him, but his hands clutched at a willow along shore and, luckily, the cane held. From then on, the current could only tug ineffectually, and he was able to crawl cold and dripping onto the brushy bank.

For a long time he lay at the edge of the river, hacking from the water in his lungs, too exhausted to drag himself further.

When he was able to sit up, he took off his pack and laid the soggy contents to dry. The meat was wet but not ruined, and his bow and arrows, which had been tied securely to the pack, were intact, as were his snares. But his axe was gone, lost for all time in the deep, dark race of the river. No longer could he cut wood for fires or blaze trees to mark his passing.

He tried to swallow a bit of meat for strength, but his throat was raw from choking, and he ended up sucking on the meat until the flavor was gone. He would have liked to lie stretched out in the sunshine, but he was worried about Rusty, who had been carried downstream by the current.

He started down the bank and was just in time to find Rusty trotting faster and faster through the brush, followed by a huge gray wolf. "Arrrk!" Rusty croaked, looking back over his shoulder nervously. As the wolf saw David he faded into the brush. Clearly the northern forest was no place for a flightless young whooping crane to wander alone.

With Rusty close upon his heels, David made his way upstream to a point across the river from the launching site. For a moment he stood staring at the last blaze he had made, shining like a bright star on the trunk of a black spruce. Then, sighting back as best he could and marking his trail either by broken branches or by small blazes cut with his pocketknife, he journeyed on.

Atop a small rise David found a large patch of mountain cranberries in possession of a family of bears. The vines were crimson with fruit. "Come on, Rusty!" David called and rushed forward shouting, with Rusty flapping his wings mightily as he trotted along behind. Together they made such a fearsome sight that the bears back off for a moment, stared, then fled, stopping now and then to stand on their hind legs to peer back at the intruders. After feasting on tart berries until they could eat no more, David stretched out in the sun for a few moments to rest.

So often had David's ears played tricks on him that he scarcely listened anymore for the sounds of planes. Thus it was Rusty who picked up a new murmur in the distance, cocked his head, then rose to his feet listening intently. For a moment David watched him curiously, then he too got up to listen. In the distance he heard a throbbing drone, fading away only to recur again, louder now and more persistent. Perhaps it was the river—but no, it came from the opposite direction.

As the sound grew ever louder, David sprinted out into the open patch of cranberries, leaving the confused bird to trail along behind. Suddenly in the distance he saw a light observation plane, such as those used by fire fighters, heading directly toward the clearing not far above the tops of the trees. Outside of the giant jets flying the upper atmosphere, it was the first plane David had seen since the crash.

Scampering forward, he leaped into the air and shouted, without the slightest doubt that the pilot was staring down at him. Rusty, mistaking these antics perhaps for a dance connected somehow with the arrival of the strange noisy bird overhead, flapped his wings and joined the fun.

For a moment David felt sure the pilot had seen him, for the plane bore left as though starting to bank and circle for a better look. Then, to his agony, the plane corrected its course and flew on, continuing on its way. How very stupid he had been! He had run directly beneath the plane's flight path, not realizing until too late that the pilot would have little or no visibility straight ahead and beneath and would most likely be looking at the ground on either side of his course.

For some time after the throb of the engine had died in the distance, David sat quietly on a mossy log, his head in his hands. Sensing his sadness, the young whooping crane stood idly by. The boy felt like crying but the tears wouldn't come. Putting his arm about the bird, he buried his face in the softness of Rusty's feathers.

Twelve

AS the days grew shorter, there was a scent of autumn in the air. Early morning frosts nipped the land, painting the shrubbery a riot of crimson and yellow, turning the tamaracks to blazing gold. Instead of causing the northern berries, such as cowberries, to wither on their stems, however, it seemed only to sweeten them. David could seldom resist stopping to pick a choice handful whenever he passed them along the trail.

His jacket was hardly warm enough to keep off the chill of darkness, so as evening came he would put on Archie's big jacket, even though it hung on him like a tent. To make a blanket, he began hoarding the skins of hares and tied them into a crude sort of robe. Kise had softened and tanned skins by rubbing them with raw brains, as the Indians had done, but David had no time. The blanket remained so stiff and crackly it woke the creatures of the forest whenever he rolled over in the night.

Snug in his bed of sphagnum moss, covered by his robe and Archie's coat, he lay looking up at northern skies, brilliant with clouds of stars. At times he forgot his predicament and thought himself the luckiest boy alive to be wandering alone with a pal like Rusty, one of the last whooping cranes on earth, and with no grownups around to take credit for what he was accomplishing in the way of survival. When the wind howled down off the arctic barrens, he turned his back to the storm, made a shelter of spruce boughs heaped high with moss, buried his nose in his robe, and with Rusty flopped down beside his bed, was pleasantly warm.

David dreaded the day when Rusty must inevitably fly and leave him earthbound as he explored the upper air. Something Archie had said once miles back in time now came winging back to haunt him. "When the time comes, David, we won't be able to keep him; we'll have to let him go."

And of course Archie was right. If winter caught them still in the wilderness, there would be nothing for Rusty to eat and he would surely die. The bird was grown now, with wings fully feathered, yet never once had Rusty tried to fly. If eventually the crane had to migrate, David realized that he had better start now to practice flying so that his wings would be strong enough for such an ordeal. And since Rusty hadn't yet started to fly on his own, David also realized that he might just have to teach him.

Whenever they came to a suitable clearing, David spread his arms and ran flapping into the wind with Rusty chasing after, working his wings as though trying to get airborne. At first it was David who—fingers spread like pinion feathers, feeling the wind, dashing across the meadows in great, happy, broad jumps— could travel through the air the farthest. "If only I could fly," he thought on these occasions. "How easy it would be, then, to find my way."

Little by little, however, as Rusty's long wings became strong with exercise, his attempts were even more spectacular than David's, and soon he became the undisputed champion. Suddenly it was the crane who became the teacher, tugging at David's clothes, running on ahead, wings flapping, trying to teach David what seemed ridiculously simple. After a ground-skimming flight of several hundred feet, the crane would always land and stroll back to the boy.

One afternoon as the crane was feeding on cowberries and had allowed the boy to wander ahead, Rusty glanced up from his plundering to see the great yellow eyes of a lynx staring at him through a bush. With a horrendous squawk Rusty opened his wings and made a dash to catch up with David.

Springing free from cover, the huge gray cat bounded after. Closer and closer it came, gaining with each long-legged bound. David heard Rusty's squawk of terror and rushed back. He saw the situation and knew he couldn't possibly arrive in time to help.

"Fly, Rusty, fly!" he shouted.

As though struck by some age-old instinct, Rusty turned suddenly into the wind, flapped his wings heavily, and the breeze lifted him into the air just as the cat sprang. Its razor claws slashed murderously, but brought down only a puff of feathers as the animal fell back and gathered himself to spring again. Higher and higher the crane sailed as the lynx, thwarted, spat sullenly at the onrushing boy.

"Scat!" David shouted. He caught the cat in the ribs with a flung stick, and the animal bounded into the trees and was gone.

For a time the crane flew on, so excited to be flying that he seemed to forget David. "Hey, Rusty! Come on down!" David called. But Rusty vanished over a grove of aspens. He had learned to fly straight ahead, but had not mastered the turn.

David sat on a log and waited. "Stupid bird!" he muttered. He wanted to be on his way, but his only chance of seeing Rusty again in this vast wilderness was for the crane to come back looking for him. He had to stay put.

A flock of blackbirds flying in a leaderless, shapeless blob whirled down out of the sky, foraged for a few moments, then took nervously to the air again and disappeared, leaving the glade even lonelier than before. He wondered if Rusty would ever learn to turn or if he would fly in a straight line until he could remain airborne no longer and fell into some distant polar sea. Loneliness fell over him like a damp shroud, and fear and despair followed. "Come back, Rusty! Come back!" he shouted to the winds, then muttered to himself, "Alone I'll never get out of this mess. Never!" A cold breeze blew out of the north, sending a flurry of golden aspen leaves down about him to blanket the ground.

He moved into the forest for a few yards, then came back again, wracked with indecision. He had to proceed, yet he couldn't go on without Rusty. What if the bird did return and found the glade empty and him gone? What if the lynx came back and found Rusty resting in the meadow, exhausted from his flight? It would be all over in seconds.

David was watching so intently in the direction in which Rusty had disappeared that he scarcely heard the rush of wings behind him as Rusty swept in over the trees, long legs trailing clumsily as though he still had no idea of where to carry them while in flight.

"Slow down!" David shouted, jumping up and down in his excitement. Unused to landing, the crane came in much too fast. To avoid being demolished, David fell on the ground, while the crane landed in a tangle of golden tamaracks.

"Awk!" he called, as though chortling over his endeavor.

Carefully David inspected him for injuries, but aside from looking as though some of his feathers had been stuck on backward, the young whooper seemed none the worse for his experience.

David gave his pal a hug, took his pack, and together once again, they moved on, with Rusty trailing along behind as patiently as ever.

But the flight had been a breakthrough for the bird, and soon he began taking longer and longer journeys through the air. At first his landings looked so much like crashes that David covered his eyes rather than watch, but in time Rusty learned to brake his forward motion with his broad wings and to use his long legs as shock absorbers.

All David had to do to send Rusty airborne was to run with his arms outstretched and flapping. Then the crane would come chasing after, flying easily over the boy's head and away. Sometimes his flights carried him afar over the land until he was but a speck in the distance, but always he returned, skimming the trees until he found David, piping and chortling with humor and affection as though to share with the earthbound his new-found joys.

Without his axe to blaze his way, David had become more and more careless about leaving signs to mark his passage, and soon after leaving the river he abandoned marking the trees entirely in his hurry to be on. There were times, however, when he missed the assurance the blazes had given him. Now and again he passed glades that bore a distinct resemblance to some he had passed before, and groves of aspen trees that were hauntingly familiar. He was filled often now with a recurrent sort of terror that he was lost and wandering in circles. He slept less and less during the lengthening nights and the heavy frosts of morning found him in a frenzy to be on.

In late September he saw his first black and white ptarmigan, which had migrated in from the barrens to the north. There were covey after covey of them, but they were so trusting and gentle he could not bear to shoot one. The plump little grouse moved a few short feet out of their way as they passed, eyeing them quizzically as though wondering how a friendship of such diverse forms as a whooping crane and a man had come to exist. Often now as he marched on, David found where a fox or owl had dined without sentiment and left only a patch of feathers scattered on the moss.

By David's estimation he had traveled almost three hundred miles, which, by Archie's reckoning, might have brought him to the Fort Smith–Hay River highway. Eagerly he watched for a human sign, listened for trucks in the distance, consulted his tattered maps, figured and refigured his position. But something happened, one day, to put his navigation to shame.

As he moved through a dried bog, his heart leaped when he saw human footprints in the raw dirt. Stale as they were, he was ready to follow them when, suddenly, the tracks joined those of a large crane and the two proceeded together. The tracks were his own, made several weeks before! Without the aid of the blazes he had done what many a woodsman had done before him. He had wandered in a circle.

For a time David sat on a log and tried to put his thoughts together. His poor head whirled and the only directions he knew for sure were those of the ground and sky. A chill wind blew down from the north as if to remind him of his desperate plight. So little time before the snow came. So little time. Impatient to be on, Rusty croaked to him and flapped his wings, but David sat still, his coat drawn tightly about him, his head sagging, his chin cupped in his hands.

When the cold was no longer bearable, he rose and beat the circulation back into his body by stamping his feet and thumping his arms against his sides. Once more the instinct for survival welled within and he moved on.

In order to get a better view of his surroundings, he picked an aspen taller than the rest and climbed to the top while Rusty eyed him curiously from the ground and even flew over him to inspect his progress, as though he suspected that David was about to launch himself from the treetop to learn to fly.

He was closer to the big river than he had imagined; in the distance he caught the shine of water, and when the wind changed, he could hear the roar of rapids. Then his heart skipped a beat as over the ocean of treetops he made out a small hill rising above the plain, lording it over the surrounding forests.

It was the first hill he had seen since the crash, and the sight excited him since the summit might give him a good view of the terrain. Carefully noting its position, he swung down through the limbs of the tree and lined out through the thick woods.

STRANGE COMPANION

The slopes of the hill were cloaked with thickets of spruce and tamarack, and Rusty took to his wings rather than fight the tangles. He circled high above, calling to David whenever he caught sight of him in the clearings. Here and there were beds where moose and buffaloes had sought summer refuge from insects. Spruce grouse gaped at David in surprise, and walked foolishly along the needled branches for a better view of the intruder.

Once he had gained the bare, fire-scarred summit, and his friend had landed safely beside him, David stood gazing across the distant forests for a sign of smoke or for the straight, unnatural scars a road makes on the terrain. There were only the skeins of buffalo trails, crossing and recrossing each other haphazardly and heading nowhere. From such a distance the river looked smooth and innocent, with no indication of its vicious nature. Then, suddenly, almost hidden by trees at the edge of a large open glade he saw a small cabin.

His heart skipped wildly, and he grabbed the startled crane with a wild bear hug. "Hey, Rusty! You see what I see? A cabin! And where there's a cabin there are bound to be people! Let's go!"

The distance was too great to see if smoke was rising from the chimney, but he took a good bearing ahead and plunged down the hill, scattering game as he ran. Grouse thundered away in terror; a cow moose stamped at him defiantly, sniffed her grown twins, then circled the hill and was gone. Rusty cruised overhead, circling easily to slow his own forward progress to David's pace. As though he sensed his friend's excitement, the crane piped happily.

In descending, David soon lost sight of the meadow, but by keeping the slopes to his back and cruising a straight line through the forest, he soon came out into the clearing he sought. In the opening a herd of cow buffaloes with big weanling calves panicked at his approach and rumbled into the brush. Rusty landed at his feet and followed him out into the glade.

Suddenly among a grove of aspens he saw the cabin. He shouted and the trees echoed his "halloo," but the door stayed shut and the little windows stared with unblinking gaze. There was no sign of smoke, no indication of life at all.

David approached cautiously, feeling somehow that he was intruding upon the cabin's loneliness. Hanging from the eaves a rusty double-bitted axe, its handle warped and moss-encrusted, showed that no one had used the cabin in some time. The door was warped and stuck; it took all of David's strength to open it. The rusty hinges squalled as if to summon help.

Inside a salt-hungry porcupine had gnawed away part of the sill; squirrels had made a nest in the heap of brown spruce boughs the former tenant had used for a bed. On the table there was a knife, its blade broken, and some empty tin cans, but the cupboard was open and bare of food. Hanging from the rafters was a crosscut saw and a bundle of traps, mostly broken. There were two rustic chairs of white-barked birch, bottomed and backed with strips of untanned moosehide. As David opened the door of the barrel stove, a wood mouse blinked at the sudden light, then leaped to the floor and vanished through a chink between the logs.

A sudden noise behind him made him jump, but it was only Rusty, who had followed him through the open door and had pulled a tin can from the table.

"Out!" David ordered, pushing the crane out the door.

He picked up the can and stared at the colored illustration of a fat, luscious peach on the paper label. Oh, to have such a peach here in his hands to eat! The label slid from the can, fluttering to the floor, and he picked it up and pinned it to a crack in the logs with a splinter of wood, surprised at what a bit of color could do to brighten the drab grays and browns of the walls.

Suddenly he felt as though he had lived here for years. This small northern meadow, ringed with golden-leaved birches, aspens, tamaracks, and contrasting dark, sculptured spruces, seemed to him as lovely a spot as any he had seen. He had found the cabin just in time. Winter would be soon upon the land, and he knew his best chances for survival lay in holing up in the cabin and toughing out the snows until spring.

He built a fire of parched, brown spruce needles from the bed. From the snapping, crackling flames an orange glow came through the open door of the crude barrel stove and pooled and danced upon the split logs of the floor. He stood close, soaking up the heat, happier and more content than he had been in some time.

But a few minutes of idleness was enough. From a neighboring thicket he cut some birch twigs, which he bound into a serviceable broom, and while Rusty hovered at the door, swept the floor bachelor clean. The squirrels, who had been the cabin's most recent occupants, darted in across the rafters, peered down at him in astonishment, then decided that the out-of-doors might be safer and retreated to the roof. David grinned. He did not in the least mind sharing the abode with squirrels, but there would have to be a few rules about dividing the food supplies.

It was hard for Rusty to understand why he had been excluded from the cabin. He paced the front of the log house, croaking pathetically in his loneliness, and soon David had to weaken and let him in, where he proved his worth by chasing away the mice that danced in and out of the cracks in the wood floor.

"You're better than a cat any old day, Rusty," David laughed, and the crane croaked happily as he probed a crack with his long, sharp beak.

Gathering moss from the surrounding forest, David made a soft two-foot-thick layer in one corner of the cabin and covered it with tips of spruce boughs, which filled the cabin with their fragrance. Over this soft, springy mattress he draped his rabbit fur robe, and he placed Archie's coat at the head as a pillow.

With the broken knife he proceeded to chink the more obvious cracks between the logs with moss. Soon the fire had driven the musty, damp smell from the cabin, and the place took on the comfort and security of his little room in the gable of the old farmhouse back home.

Outside the cabin was a tower of poles some thirty feet high. Atop this tower the former owner had built a platform, a cache on which to store food safe from marauding bears and wolverines. Though the rungs of the ladder leading to the top were rotted, David managed to scramble up. As he peered over the edge of the platform, he held his breath, hoping that among the few remnant bundles of the cache there might be something of value.

The pile was covered with rotting canvas. Excitedly David pulled away the brittle, weathered fabric and found a huddle of items the previous owner had not bothered to take away. There was a shovel, useful in winter; some seasoned staves for making axe handles; a coal-oil lantern with a few extra wicks; ten gallons of coal oil; a few enamel cups and plates, chipped from rough use; five tins of matches, four rusted and the contents ruined. There were no canned foods, though in a sealed five-gallon tin David found some tea in hard blocks, like plug tobacco. Most precious of all was a small supply of lumpy salt. Starved for the taste, David put a lump on the palm of his hand and licked away until the salt was gone.

Carefully David carried his treasures down to the cabin. Rusty inspected each load, but seemed unimpressed with their value. And indeed the hoard was nothing that would have impressed anyone in civilization, but for David any useful item was a treasure.

He tried to picture his benefactor, that unknown man who years before had labored hard and long and had left a cabin and the implements of survival to whoever might come after.

Rusty seemed to sense David's joy in his new home and was already in command, an imperious watchman—patrolling the immediate vicinity of the cabin, sending the squirrels back to the roof top, and keeping the Canada jays up in their trees. Whenever David shut the cabin door against his mischief, he paced outside the walls of the building, calling endearments that, with neglect, became calls of alarm until David weakened and let the bird in. Once indoors it was only a matter of time before he pulled the pots off the table or tugged the moss out of the cracks with his probing beak.

Tired as David was from the excitement of the day, he set some snares in neighboring thickets. The rolypoly ptarmigan, which strolled casually out of their way, were already wearing their white robes of winter, and David knew that the first snow was not far off. While there was time for a few short exploratory forays through the forest, looking for signs of civilization, he knew that he must keep the cabin as a trump card, a haven within easy reach in case of storm.

That night, with Rusty safe indoors standing on one leg beside his bed, and the door barricaded against bears, David slept for the first time in months with a roof instead of stars overhead.

Thirteen

THE next day David, with Rusty at his heels, set out to explore his new domain, searching beyond the periphery of the primitive building for traces of the cabin's previous occupant. He found a few rotting stumps that had contributed logs for the construction of the cabin, or for stove wood, and in a thicket he came upon a dump of rusty cans, most weathered into a fragile lacework, but some still salvageable for use, such as storing dried foods.

For a moment he assumed that the use of canned goods, which are heavy and hard to transport on one's back, indicated that the cabin was fairly close to civilization, then he realized that most likely some bush pilot had made a food drop from a plane and thus supplied a trapper with enough food for a long winter.

High up the sides of trees he noticed blaze marks, and shook in his shoes with the scary thought that they had been made by a giant axeman, twenty feet tall. The fun suddenly went out of exploring until he realized that the blazes could have been made by a man of normal height standing on snowshoes on the winter snows.

For some distance he followed the axe marks, hoping they might lead to a village, but instead he realized from the erratic course they took through the forest that the blazes had merely marked out a trapper's winter trap line.

One blazed trail led straight to the river, indicating that the trapper had used that torrent as his highway to and from civilization. A broken canoe paddle—its handle consumed by salt-hungry porcupines, half grown into the crotch of an aspen tree—pointed to the manner of the man's travel. Not only did David lack a canoe and the skill to navigate white water alone, but he could find no clue whether the man traveled up- or downstream to reach civilization.

The boy was in a quandary. Maybe civilization was close at hand, a few miles downstream. But then again, maybe the trapper had journeyed downstream in the spring, his canoe laden with furs, and by pre-arrangement rendezvoused along the shore of Great Slave Lake with a trader or with a fuel barge plying the open waters along the shore. Neither barge nor trader would still be there. No, with winter close at hand, the boy knew that he had better not gamble, but set about trying to survive the winter in the cabin.

He was faced with another agonizing decision and that was what to do with Rusty. If he could not winter with him in the cabin, then somehow Rusty must be induced to migrate south without him. Day by day, cherishing the bird's company, he put off making up his mind, yet he knew that the decision must come soon.

The days were shorter now and there was little time to mull over such plans or feel sorry for himself. Since food and firewood would be his most critical needs for winter, he pushed himself hard to lay in supplies. Kise had warned him once that aspen gives off little heat, so he cut only dead, seasoned spruce and tamarack, which he piled close to the cabin until the woodpile loomed far larger than the building.

Once the wood was cut, he restored the tumble-down smokehouse to its former state, then laid in a supply of willow for smoking and drying meat. The privy roof he mended with shakes, thick shingles split from a bolt of tamarack, so that this vital building would not fill to the roof with snow.

One of the treasures the trapper had left behind was a coil of heavy wire for anchoring traps. From this David made some snares capable of holding big game, and set them in game trails leading to a small natural mineral lick in a nearby marsh. He anchored one end of each snare carefully to a stout sapling, choosing one that would bend at the first rush of an animal to break free, but not crack or be torn up by the roots. It was a simple trick, no more complicated than catching an arctic hare.

Early the next morning as he moved out over the frosty ground to check his snare line, he found a young cow moose lying dead in one of his sets. From the tracks he noted that she had come blundering down the trail. Feeling the noose around her neck, she had plunged to free herself, but the noose had only tightened about her, and falling back on her haunches against the wire, she had died within moments for lack of oxygen.

Frightened by the sight of the moose lying outstretched before them, Rusty squawked loudly and fled a safe distance. David feared that the wolves might find the cow, so he rushed back to camp and returned with an axe and saw. Cutting the meat into small strips to be cured, he packed load after load into camp for smoking. The hide he saved for making rawhide snowshoes and moccasins, and by nightfall only the head and scraped bones were left.

Using strips of untanned moosehide, he lashed new rungs on the ladder leading up to the cache, and as the strips of meat dried in the smokehouse, he placed them in tins to be stored high up on the platform. Every usable tin from the dump found itself back in service as a receptacle for dried berries, greens, and even lichens, or rock tripe, which he stripped from rocks for later powdering into soup. Even when David thought he had a good start toward laying in his winter supplies, he kept gathering stores like a squirrel, amassing food against the coming emergency.

A hard freeze turned the rushes tan and covered the sloughs along the river with ice, save where waterfowl kept channels open by constant cruising in the cold, still darkness. One night he stood before the cabin, shoulders hunched against the chill, and stared up at the brilliance of the starlit skies. Overhead, the ducks and geese were calling their farewells, and he listened sadly to the solemn whoopings of great white swans and the high-pitched squealings of white-fronted geese. From the forest the wolves howled mournfully and all-knowingly as though they sensed his vulnerability. He shivered with self-doubt. He had a growing food supply, a snug shelter, and fuel for cooking and warmth. But somehow fear gnawed at his bowels. Kise had told him tales of the north, where cabin fever did strange things to lonely men. Upset even by tiny, unimportant matters, a man often did desperate things.

When he could no longer stand the cold, David moved into the cabin, shutting the door against the night and stoking the fire to drive the chill from his bones. While Rusty slept, head tucked beneath his wing, David took up a piece of wood, and in the flickering light of the coal-oil lantern, whiled away the evening by whittling out a crude figure of a cow moose. He could not sleep, for troubling him was the unsettled question of what to do about Rusty.

It was almost dawn when he sought out his bed, and when he awoke he found Rusty pacing the floor in front of the door to be let out. As soon as Rusty left the cabin, he leaped into the air for his morning flight. These days the young whooping crane was spending more and more of his time in the air, circling endlessly with only occasional wing beats to keep him aloft, calling forlornly to David to join him in flight.

Often David glanced up longingly from his work to watch as the crane swept back and forth over the vast, lonely lands. If only he could fly, how quickly he would soar over the forests back to Kise and the old farm. Kise would be busy now, harvesting the late planting of oats, weaning the calves, and getting the last of the windrowed hay into the barn for winter. Perhaps there was a hired boy now to take his place, sleeping in his bed underneath the eaves. He tried to remember why he had run away, but he could recall only the good things about home. He would be four-teen soon, and that was a long way from being thirteen and a half.

The young whooping crane came in on a long glide, skimming the trees, defiantly unwilling to change his course for a flock of ducks cannonading across his path. At the last second the ducks lost their nerve, tumbled to avoid collision, then regained con-trol, quacking angrily at the crane. David watched thoughtfully as Rusty landed at his feet and ambled over to peck his shoelaces.

"You're in for a rough time, Rusty," the boy mused. "There's no way you could get by for a long winter living on the food I'd have to feed you, and there's no way you could dig down through the snow and ice covering the ponds to get your own. You hate to be left alone so much you'd beat yourself to death on the cabin door if I locked you in while I went off on snowshoes to check my snares. I guess your best chance would be to migrate south and leave me behind."

David realized that left to his own devices, due to the bond between them, Rusty would not migrate, but would stay on and on until it was too late to fight his way southward through the intense cold or the buffeting storms of winter. However much he would miss his companionship, David had to find a way to send the bird winging south.

The flight would not be easy. He pictured Rusty badgered and beaten by storms, calm and trusting as he headed over hunters dedicated to taking meat home for the pot. He thought of the other hazards Archie had mentioned—power lines, hazing aircraft, polluted streams and marshes, rodent poisons. "Of all these," Archie had said, "the danger of an ignorant, unthinking man reaching for his gun outweighs all the rest." For the first time it came home to David that Rusty would not be wild toward people but tame, and might descend at the feet of the first human he saw, mistaking him for David.

Provided Rusty lived through the encounter, what a sensation the sudden appearance of a tame whooping crane would cause! All over North America the news media would be charged with speculation as to how a young whooping crane flying in from one of the most desolate areas in the world, from a vast, uninhabited land, had come to be tame. Had he been raised by human hands, cared for by some person or persons unknown? Would any guess that far to the north, in snowbound isolation, the boy who had saved that whooping crane from death in the egg was himself in desperate need of saving?

If only Rusty could talk and tell their story. Talk? David leaped to his feet and flung his arms about the startled bird. "Rusty!" he shouted gleefully. "You can do it! You can save me! A message to the outside world. Airmail even. Why you may go down in history as the largest carrier pigeon of all time!"

As though he somehow understood, Rusty, caught up in the boy's excitement, wormed from his embrace, picked up a stick, and began to dance.

David cut a metal sheet from a tin can, then, poring over his maps, punched tiny holes in the tin with the point of his knife to show the location of the wrecked plane, the numbers on the wings, his approximate route of travel, the big river flowing north, the bald hill, the trapper's cabin, and the date as he guessed it. He included, too, Kise's name and address and the letters SOS. He held the tin up against the sky for easier reading, and satisfied it was legible, folded the tin into a leg band. Shaking in his excitement, he caught Rusty in his arms, bent the strip snugly around one of Rusty's long legs, and twisted the ends together.

Rusty glared at him indignantly. Feathers puffed up, he tried to pry off the metal with his stout bill, but the latch held firm. For the rest of the day the young crane pouted and stayed away from David, but that evening David set out some strips of moose liver, and Rusty approached, still perturbed by the band but not wanting the jays to steal his food. By nightfall he had forgotten the indignity, and as if resting for ordeals to come, slept on one leg in his favorite corner, head tucked lightly beneath his wing.

It was a sad morning for David as he walked through the northern forest with his friend for what would be the last time. The young crane was restless and soon took to the air, flying circles higher and higher into the cold, gray reaches of the sky. At times he would descend to where David played at gathering a few frozen berries and tug gently at his jacket, impatient for him to come along, giving him one more chance to learn to fly.

But as David could tell from the nervous tensions showing in the bird and from the frequent dancing leaps into the air, the instincts for migration were already gnawing hard at him. Soon Rusty was airborne once more, and the cold northern winds off the barrens buoyed him quickly aloft. David watched him go, tears streaming down his cheeks, awaiting the chance to set in motion the plan he had decided on in the night. As the crane sailed blithely behind a cathedral of a cloud, the boy plunged into a heavy thicket of spruce and lay still, hardly daring to breathe.

Sweeping back over the land, Rusty soon discovered that his friend had vanished, and called down plaintively in his aloneness. For some time, as David shivered on the ground, the whooping crane circled on high, watching for movement below. David could hear his calls of distress as they fell afar upon the land. Then, slowly, the crane's circles widened as the great bird lifted higher and higher, and soon he was lost over the vast marshes, rivers, and forests of the northland.

When, at last, he was sure that Rusty had gone, David rose stiffly to his feet and ventured out of the thicket. He looked to the horizon, hoping against hope to see Rusty, but he saw only the clouds, which had begun to lower, and already great flakes of snow were beginning to collect on his jacket. Chilled to the bone, he flailed his arms against his sides to increase circulation, glad that he had left a hearty fire burning in the stove.

As he drew near the cabin, with the changing wind came the smell of smoke. For the moment it gave him comfort, then suddenly, as he emerged from the thickets into the clearing, he saw the orange glow of fire leaping from the roof.

The smoke billowed in clouds, which were sucked away by the persistent wind. Grabbing his shovel, David leaped up onto the woodpile and then onto the roof. From the location of the fire, still limited to a section of the roof, he guessed that a spark from the chimney had ignited the moss he had piled across the roof for insulation. The acrid smoke stung his throat and took his breath away.

Despair almost conquered him. Then as he moved to safety, ready to let the fire take its course, anger swept over him like a wave. Grabbing the shovel, he attacked the fire in a fury, packing shovelfuls of dirt up over the woodpile to the roof and hurtling the contents at the flames, driving them back, smothering them down into their own smoke. The big wet snow-flakes came hissing down like allies, dampening the moss about the fire, and little by little the smoke be-gan to die and at last the fire was vanquished.

Still he worked on. As the snow whitened the rest of the roof, David dug away the blackened moss from around the chimney and replaced it with flat stones and mud so that the stovepipe was screened from all flammable material and far safer than before.

Only when the job was finished did he relax. For a long time he sat on a stump at the edge of the forest, ignoring the snowflakes clinging to his lashes or melt-ing down his cheeks. He wanted to cry, but he had a feeling the north was there like a human enemy, watching him, waiting for the first signs of weakening resolve. He realized that his survival would depend upon his ability to control his emotions, and the tears did not come. He rose from the log and walked to the cabin. The place reeked with smoke, but it was bearable. Shutting the door against the cold, he put a few split logs into the stove, and as the wind howled about the eaves, he cut a hare into small pieces, placed it in a pot made from a gallon can, and set it on the stove to boil.

Darkness fell over the land. He thought he heard Rusty tapping at the door to get in and went out for a moment, but there was nothing there. Out of the blackness above came the swirl of snowflakes. The dim light spilling from the cabin door fell upon a world of unfamiliar shapes. For a time he stood listening, hoping against hope to hear Rusty's familiar call, but the only sounds he heard were the hiss of melting snow on the hot stovepipe and the swish and thump of snow-laden branches as they dumped their burden on the ground below.

Fourteen

MOVING in from the north, the cold, heavy air mass caught Rusty's broad wings, and like a runaway kite, he soared quickly skyward, up, up, up into thin upper air. For a time the young crane skirted the fringes of iron-gray clouds built in mist factories over arctic seas, peering curiously into fluffy caverns, floating now above, now below, the churning mass. Perhaps he looked for David, half expecting to find his friend hiding there, playing hide-and-seek as he had done along the trail on many a summer day.

Until now the bird had been flying with long legs trailing. As the leg band began to contract and draw tight with cold, Rusty tucked his legs forward beneath the soft, warm feathers of his abdomen, much as a plane draws up its landing gear. His frequent calls of loneliness and distress were lost in that vast abyss.

Far below him scattered flocks of white-fronted, Canada, and snow geese, beating their way south. He had no impulse to join the groups. His parents had been Archie and David, and thus imprinted, Rusty could only have imagined himself as human in form. If he searched for others of his kind in the skies, he looked not for other cranes but for human beings.

The young whooping crane was soon hungry. For several days the marshes near the cabin had been bound with ice, and he had eaten only frozen berries and seeds or what food he gleaned from those areas kept open by geese and swans. Now as he flew, his body consumed his reserve of fatty tissues, releasing enzymes into his bloodstream that further triggered the age-old drive of migration.

Lonely as he was, he did not settle to earth, but spent his first night aloft, helplessly following his instincts, and drifted southward. In a few hours he passed over the entire distance he had walked with David and swept on beyond. Perhaps as he floated over clustered lights of the first towns on the Canadian prairie, he saw them only as reflections of brilliant stars on quiet water.

When, at last, Rusty gave in to hunger and fatigue and trailed downward, it was daylight, and already he was in southern Saskatchewan. For a time he waded a small marsh, probing the shallows among flocks of waterfowl until he had eaten and drunk his fill, then strolled into the stubble fields bordering the marsh for a dessert of wheat kernels, fallen at harvest time from some farmer's inefficient combine.

Now and again large flocks of noisy geese and squealing, gabbling ducks came winging in to the pond at the center of the marsh to rest and drink, then took off again for the wheat fields to glean grain. For several days Rusty moped about the marsh, glancing frequently toward the skies as though he expected David to catch up.

It was on his last day at this resting area that Rusty became a matter of public record. The sanctuary he had chosen happened to be part of the wildlife refuge at the north end of Last Mountain Lake in Saskatchewan, a frequent stopping place for whooping cranes on their way south from Wood Buffalo Park. The refuge manager had closed his records on migrating whoopers for the year and was startled to sight a lone, immature whooping crane on the marsh so late in the season. Within minutes the manager had contacted refuge headquarters on his car radio, and word that one more whooping crane was still heading south, and might be added to the tally of living birds, was flashing south to agents along the whooping crane flyway, to the Endangered Species Research Center in Patuxent, Maryland, and to refuge headquarters at Aransas.

A carload of interested scientists from the Museum of Natural History at Regina arose before dawn and braved the cold prairie winds to look for the crane, but they were too late. During the night a weather front had moved a mass of arctic air southward, turning the ponds to ice. On all of Rusty's marsh the only open water was a patch in the deeper area where a family of swans had cruised out the darkness and kept the ice from forming. Even Last Mountain Lake lay under glass and had seen its last wave for the winter.

The storm brought a restlessness to all the birds. Just before dawn the swans departed ghostlike into the drifting fogs, and soon the crane took wing, circling higher and higher into the air as though uncertain of direction. When, once again, the earth lay in miniature beneath him, he turned with a favorable current of wind and let it carry him southward.

Another night fell. The winds blustered and plucked at his feathers, but hurtled him on his way. A flight of goldeneyes, wings whistling silvery music, swept past him. Lines of geese and swans plodded southward, keeping contact with each other in the darkness with constant vocal soundings.

It was over the Dakotas that Rusty glimpsed, through parting cumulus, a scattering of small cattail-bordered marshes that attracted him. Ahead of him a flock of wing-weary Canada geese saw the marshes too and banked sharply to descend a stairwell of sunshine down through the mists. Perhaps because the sky above the clouds was suddenly empty without them, Rusty followed them down.

Below him the wary Canadas made a wide sweep of the land, inventorying every detail, watching for danger, eyeing the grain field there, the pond beneath, for the telltale gleam of light from gun barrels or a hunter's upturned face to warn them away.

Three times the Canadas circled the pond with Rusty close behind. Then suddenly, as they let the wind slip through their pinions and glided low, from the rushes along the shore came the roar of guns. Whump! Whump! Whump! Puffs of smoke rose from the brittle tan rushes and drifted away. Ahead of Rusty two Canadas crumpled, their beauty erased forever, and plummeted down, sending up twin geysers of spray. A black retriever charged from the vegetation, hit the water with a splash, and swam toward the floating birds. Gabbling in terror, the surviving geese beat heavily on creaking wings to gain elevation.

Whump! Whump! Rusty felt a sudden sharp pain in one wing, and as he tried desperately to climb, wind hissed through a gap in his feathers. Even the clumsy geese were fast leaving him behind. Lower and lower he flew until suddenly he was clipping the cattails with his breast—puffs of cattail fuzz floated like tiny clouds across the marsh—and he fell into the brown sea of rushes, where he lay, with wings outstretched, gasping for his life.

Near him a pair of golden retrievers crashed through the rushes toward where they had marked him down. Vaguely aware that they were the enemy, Rusty froze, head lowered in the reeds. He could hear rather than see them as they beat the brittle rushes down with their chests, searching in a frenzy for the game, which had to be maddeningly close.

The cattail fuzz drifted like a small blizzard across the marsh.

Rusty drew his wings to his sides and waited. His tan and white feathers camouflaged him well among the cattails, but the dogs made a circle through the rushes and came upwind, moving a bit slower now as though puzzled by the strange scent. Through the forest of rushes Rusty suddenly caught sight of their great shaggy heads, slavering mouths, and dripping, mud-bespattered chests.

The two dogs spotted him at once and rushed in for the capture. In desperation Rusty lashed out with his saber bill and caught the first dog in the nose, then flapped his huge wings and slashed the second dog with his sharp toenails. The surprised dogs skidded to a stop. Rusty hissed like a snake and slashed again with his murderous beak. One astonished dog yipped in real pain and fled with the other close at his heels. For a time Rusty could hear them beating the marsh, whipping back and forth looking for gentler prey. The crane lay still, exhausted from his effort. Soon whistles blew over the marsh recalling the dogs to the blinds, and Rusty lay quiet, head tucked under his wing in sleep.

A week passed, and the dried blood on his wing turned from crimson to a rusty-black stain. Snow covered the marshes, and still the bird lay quiet, getting moisture from the snow to cool his fevered throat. Without food Rusty's body lost weight, and his breast became concave and hollowed. When he managed to stand, his long, stiltlike legs wobbled uncertainly, and after a few brief attempts to find food along the margins of the marsh, he was forced to rest again. The ducks and geese had left the marshes, and the ponds and grain fields were silent of the sounds of hunters' guns.

On the eighth day after his accident, as the crane was probing along a mouse run with his beak, he caught a vole and swallowed the fat mouse whole. With the warmth and strength of this unexpected food diffusing through his body, Rusty moved out from his hiding place and fed along the margins of the marsh, probing the hidden mouse runs in the hope of finding more food; but the mice were hidden deep in their burrows, and when darkness came he had added only one small mouse to his gather.

That night the storms came out of the north with a new fury, and the willows and cottonwoods along the marsh groaned under the assault.

Spreading his broad wings, Rusty turned into the wind, fingering the sweep of storm winds with his pinions, until a sudden icy blast lifted him into the air and he was airborne once more, more gliding than flying, riding a north wind south across the land.

His wing ached. As often as he gained elevation, he lost it, and he flew on barely clearing the trees. From the ominous clouds scudding above, pellets of ice caromed off his feathers. Beneath him were small fields and such animals grazing as he had never seen in the north. He wanted desperately to land again, but the animals frightened him, and he flew on into the night.

By morning he had outraced the southward movement of the snow, and the ground below him was bare, but still he rode the winds as though afraid that if he landed he could not get airborne again. But as he swooped low over a stubble field, tempted by the chance of finding grain, he circled again and gave a rusty croak. There ahead of him, strolling along a dirt road, he thought he saw his friend, David. Long legs trailing, wings beating stiffly, he lost elevation and swept in to land beside a confused and startled farm boy.

Despite the pain in his wing Rusty seized a straw, tossed it high, and bowed and leaped high in a clumsy but joyous crane dance, while the boy fled in terror.

For a moment Rusty watched him in confusion, then, thinking the boy was playing games, he spread his wings, and half flying, half running, went chasing after. Across the field they went, on past a weathered barn and right up to the farmhouse.

Had the door not slammed in his face, Rusty would have followed right into the house. He heard shouts from inside. "Hey, ma! pa! C'mere. A big bird's after me!"

Thumps and bumps indoors. Curtains fluttered in the windows as cautious faces peeped out. Rusty stood on the front porch perched on one leg, preening his wounded wing carefully with his beak as though trying to outline the hurt.

Slowly the front door of the farmhouse creaked open, out came the barrel of a shotgun through the crack, and the gun clicked threateningly as it was cocked, ready to fire. Cautiously a tall, thin-faced farmer slipped out the door, holding his gun pointed and ready before him. Rusty looked him over, croaked a pleasant greeting, and went on preening his feathers.

"Well I'll be!" the man mused. "The kid wasn't funnin' me after all. There is a bird out here. A whooping crane to boot. Ain't been one around here since grandma had her own teeth."

Suddenly he noticed the band on Rusty's leg. "Look at that, eh!" he remarked. "Somebody's marked him. You kids stay tight in the house so's you won't scare him away, and I'll slip down to the barn for a can of wheat. Wouldn't surprise me none he's somebody's pet and maybe they'll pay money for him back."

Pet or not, the grownup held his shotgun ready as he sidled past and headed for the barn. Rusty left off preening to follow behind. The farmer had that "going to get food" manner about him the crane had come to watch for in David, and he stood expectantly outside the barn while the man disappeared into the dark, musty interior. In a moment he returned with a can of wheat, which he scattered on the ground. Rusty croaked happily, sent a big brown leghorn rooster fleeing from the grain with a well-aimed peck, and began feeding right at the farmer's feet.

As though embarrassed by the shotgun cradled in his arms, Rusty's new acquaintance unloaded it, placed the shells in his pocket, and leaned the weapon against the barn. His sharp eyes missed nothing—the dried rusty medallion of blood on the crane's wing, and the way the band had been clumsily wrought and crudely fastened, not in the manner of a professional bird bander, but as by a man who lacked tools. Whoever had made a pet of the crane had clearly not been a scientist making a study. During fall migrations nowadays he often saw marked geese wearing metal leg bands, with colorful neck collars or dyed feathers or streamers fastened to their wings, decorated by man to aid in migration studies. This band looked almost as though it had been fashioned by some northern Indian or Eskimo.

As the bird fed, the man reached out gingerly and touched his plumage, then, slowly, when Rusty did not appear to care, he slid his hands downward. With a quick twist of his strong fingers, he stole the band away.

Rusty flinched and flapped his wings, then discovering that he was no longer encumbered by the band, returned quite contentedly to his feeding, even ignoring the children, who could stand the excitement no longer and had come flooding from the house.

"What was it, pa? What'd you get off his leg?"

"Piece of tin is all," the man said, "and rusty at that."

He unrolled the metal and glanced at the holes. "Piece of tin with some words punched in it," he went on, holding it up to the light. "Got an address on it from Edmonton, Alberta, and a name—Kise or something. This bird's a long way from home."

Once more he tried to decipher the writing, but could not make out the map. He fingered the metal thoughtfully, almost threw it away, then folded it again and slid it into his pocket.

"What are you going to do with the bird, pa?" a little girl asked. "Could we keep him for a pet?"

"Don't reckon I know just what to do. Call the game warden, I guess, and tell him we got a whooping crane." A frown crossed his brow as he thought of the excitement the news would cause. Half the folks in town would come flooding out, and he hoped they'd stay out of his muddy fields planted with winter wheat. And not ask him lots of stupid questions. He thought maybe it would be best just not to mention the crane at all, then he shrugged and headed toward the house to use the phone.

Fifteen

IN his kitchen the farmer cranked the magneto on the wall-hung telephone. "Operator?" His was one of the last single-wire, ground-return rural lines left in the state, and he had to shout to make himself heard, but to him the fact that the system worked at all made it more wondrous than any dial phone in town.

"Can I help you?"

"Say, operator. Get me that federal game warden over to Turnbridge Wells. Tim Garratt." He heard the operator ringing and rested the heavy ear piece for a moment until he heard a male voice on the other end of the line. "Garratt? My name is McFeeters. I farm out by the Corners. Maybe you know the place.

Reason I called is I got a tame whooping crane in my barnyard I'm feeding. Read something you wrote about the whooping cranes in the newspaper last spring and thought you might like to know. Do I know what one looks like? Hell, yes, I know. Just like this one. Big long beak. Stands chest high to a grown man. White with rusty-brown markings and kind of a black mustache on his face. And one thing more. Looks to me like he might have hurt his wing, so bring some medicine. About an hour? That's soon enough. Good-bye." The farmer clanked the ear piece down on its hook. Some ways he wished he hadn't told anyone the crane was there; could be it'd bring a lot of city folk climbing his fences; there'd been lots of stuff lately in newspapers and on radio about whooping cranes, and folks might rush out to have a look. Muttering, he moved to the door of the house and stood looking down across the yard toward where Rusty still fed on grain beside the barn.

As it turned out, the farmer was justified in his fears. Garratt's wife told a friend, who called the local radio station, and the news that a mysteriously tame whooping crane had descended from nowhere to a Dakota barnyard burst like a dropped watermelon on the small rural community. At the sight of a caravan of automobiles descending upon his privacy along the gravel road from town, the farmer locked his front gate and reloaded his shotgun against any well-meaning gawkers who might frighten the young crane away. He intended to release the bird only into the custody of Garratt, the federal warden, who would reward him with money if he had it coming and would see to it, maybe, that the wounded bird got a nice ride the rest of the way to Texas by government plane.

Waiting for the arrival of the warden, the crowd stood thronging his front gate, looking off across the fields for a glimpse of the bird.

"Probably just one of them blue herrings," someone outside the gate remarked, since blue herons were common to the area. The chuckle running through the crowd angered the farmer and awakened a stubborn determination to prove them wrong.

At the moment of the arrival of the first automobile the great amber crane, unaware of celebrity status, was engaged in devastating a dung pile below the cow shed in search of lowly earthworms or undigested grain. His wings were rested, outside of a certain stiffness where he had been shot, and he had dined well. It was probably not the rumble of approaching automobiles but a restless thirst for water that sent him airborne again.

No one saw Rusty go. He merely spread his wings and stepped into the wind, following the lowlands and watching for the shine of open water, where he might drink and preen.

It was one of the farmer's sons who betrayed his father to the crowd. The boy had peered around the corner of the shed, where the bird had last been seen, made a quick appraising survey of the surrounding fields, and rushed up the hill to the gate with the news, "Hey, pa! The bird is gone!"

This news coincided with the arrival of the warden's pickup truck and seemed to relieve the crowd of any qualms they felt about crossing the farmer's property lines. For some minutes they milled around the farm like hounds who have lost the scent, wandering aimlessly in small groups, feeling perhaps that the farmer had made fools of them and had never really seen a whooping crane at all. Soon they drifted back to the gate, where McFeeters, who had given up trying to hold back the crowd, now approached the warden by his truck.

"Reckon he took off, warden," the farmer apologized lamely.

"Reckon he took off!" snorted a man in the group. "Reckon he was just seein' things."

McFeeters's fist clutched angrily upon the rusty tin in his jacket pocket. The marks on that tin would prove that there had actually been a crane in his barnyard! Or would they? Maybe they would only laugh at him more when he claimed to have touched a whooping crane with his bare hands and removed a band someone had made from a rusty tin can.

The warden sighed. Trouble with most people was they really didn't know a crane from a goose or a heron, and the sight of any light-colored bird excited their fancies. "Thanks anyway for calling, McFeeters. If he comes back, let me know." This was the fourth false sighting he had looked into this month, and investigation had produced one whistling swan, one snow goose, and two blue herons, but no whooping cranes. It was no small wonder his thanks as he left failed to ring true.

The farmer glared at the departing townsfolk, and his son shared his indignation. "Why didn't you tell them off, pa? Show them that band you took off the leg?"

McFeeters shrugged, his thin face pinching into a frown. "They'd never have believed unless they saw the bird with their own eyes. If I'd shown them that rusty metal with holes in it and told them it came off a crane's leg, they'd just have hoorahed me more."

He took the band from his jacket and tossed it on a dusty ledge in the barn, where it was soon forgotten among a heap of rusty draft horseshoes.

As to Rusty, once he had watered on a sandbar in a river, he felt the urge to be on. He took to the air, and each turning into the wind screwed him ever higher until once more he sailed above the clouds. Beyond a certain affinity for the south, he had nothing to direct him to the Aransas Refuge marshes, where, save for chance stragglers like himself, other whooping cranes had already gathered for the winter.

For two days and nights he flew. Sometimes in the darkness he heard the flutter of soft wings as he moved through flocks of migrating songbirds, which were steering by the stars. But flocks of geese were scarce, for many had already found wintering grounds along the way and needed go no farther south.

One afternoon as he rose above the clouds with an upsweeping thermal lifting him like a friendly hand beneath each wing, he heard a vague troubling sound in the distance. "Kerloo! Kerloo!" High above him a white speck circled. He cocked his head to look, but for the moment there was nothing to connect the shining object with the call.

"Kerloo! Kerloo! Kerleoo!" The great bugling sound again, and some vague excitement stirred in Rusty's breast. He tried to trumpet, but from his long throat came only a froglike croak.

But the great bird above him must have understood, for in slow, lazy circles, letting slip the wind, it began to lower until both birds floated in the same plane, matching wing beats as they sailed on.

As naturally as Rusty had first learned to drink, he fell behind the old whooping crane, content to let it lead the way. That night they rested on a sandbar along a winding river, and fed shoulder to shoulder in the shallows on crayfish as though they had known each other always. It was as though Rusty, in delivering David's message to civilization, had paid the debt incurred in his raising and now was free to be a whooping crane.

Four days later, at Aransas Refuge, the same pilot who had escorted Rusty's parents from the refuge flew at a leisurely pace along the northern edge of the refuge. He was happy to be back. The monotony of crop-dusting, with its constant turns, takeoffs, and landings, had bored him, and as fall had come, his thoughts had drifted more and more from his crop-dusting to Aransas Refuge and the whooping cranes. Suddenly he had an irresistible craving to be back counting the cranes in after their summer in the north. He knew that even now refuge personnel would be busy getting the place ready for the arrival of the whoopers and their young, working long hours to finish projects, such as food plantings in those areas that would be off limits once the birds arrived. He was sitting in his pickup eating his lunch in far-off Mississippi when news came over the radio that the first group of the great white birds had arrived at Aransas after more than half a year's absence. He hadn't bothered to finish his sandwich, but had turned things over to his brother, and two days later, when the second group of cranes had arrived, he was back flying the observation plane and spotting them as they began their glide in to their own favorite territory on one of the sloughs.

Now as he flew his daily census flight over the refuge, he noted two specks in the sky far to the north and watched them with growing excitement as more and more they began to resemble whooping cranes.

His radio crackled with static as he flipped it on and called in the news. "Piper 139 to Headquarters!"

"Headquarters. Come in, 139."

"Hang on to your hats! Couple of late comers just straggled in. One white bird with young of the year."

"Headquarters to 139. We read you. Just got a call from the Audubon Society biologist from his blind. He's got your birds in his glasses. Thinks they're headed for that vacant territory over by Mustang Slough. Hold a minute. Yeah, they've dropped down in and landed in shallow water along the slough. You can go on with your census now and thanks. Forty-four and forty-five are home safe. Over and out."

The pilot adjusted his course. Ahead of him he could see pair seven as two snowlike patches, feeding contentedly in their marsh. Over his shoulder he could see the new arrivals, wading along the shore, getting used to the scene, poking in the water now and then to find a dinner of blue crab.

Sixteen

JUST seven days after Rusty's departure autumn ended abruptly as a fierce storm came howling down out of the north. For a time there were only wild, erratic winds, tossing the limbs of the black spruces, wresting the last golden needles from the tamaracks, and sending the game into sanctuary in the deepest thickets. Then as daylight began to wane, giant fluffy flakes came winging down from the lowering belly of the clouds.

As David watched the snows whirl in, he realized suddenly that by morning his snare line would be buried deep in snow and lost to him. Throwing Kise's big sheepskin-lined jacket about his shoulders, he rushed out through the muted forest, gathering snares as he found them until darkness forced him home. He hit the meadow a hundred yards higher than he intended. The world looked unfamiliar, and he almost panicked in fear he had lost his way. Luckily the collapse of logs in the cabin stove sent a shower of sparks into the night air to guide him back.

When he reached home, he was panting from exertion, and even as he slumped against the friendly logs, his heart still pounded. He realized that Rusty's calm presence had been a constant reassurance to him and that now, with the crane gone, he must be careful not to panic.

For a time David stood outside, shoulders hunched against the cold, taking one last look at the ground that was still bare under the shelter of the caves; by morning it would be buried deep in snow. Then, shivering with the chill, he crept into his abode, added wood to the fire, removed his sweaty garments, and sat hugging the stove, watching the flickering orange firelight dancing on his bare skin and listening to the sputter of melting snow as it leaked down the outside of the stovepipe and sizzled away in steam.

Sounds of the wind muttering about the eaves became increasingly muted as the snow laid down its heavy blanket, and he heard the roof logs creak as they adjusted to increasing strain. Proud of his snug little cabin, he stretched out comfortably on his bed of moss and boughs, covered himself with his robes, and slept.

He awoke well into the next day, and propped on

one elbow, listened for whatever sound it was that had awakened him. He thought he heard noises at the door like the sound of fluttering of feathers Rusty made when he preened. "Rusty!" he shouted and rushed from his bed. He flung open the cabin door expecting to see the crane standing there, but there was nothing. He decided the sound must have come from overladen boughs dropping their burden of snow upon the pack beneath. He stared out into a new world. The snow came to his knees, and still the storm raged, filling a familiar world with strange shapes. He had planned many a project for the day, but there was little he could do but close the cabin door and wait out the storm.

Sitting idly on a block of firewood near the stove, his mind was a whirl of questions. Where was Rusty now? Had he managed to head south before the storm arrived or had it destroyed him? Supposing the bird had escaped the wild winds, keeping ahead of the front, was it too soon to hope that the authorities had discovered the tame crane and deciphered the leg band and were now only waiting out the storm to rescue him?

He missed Rusty's company. He could see him standing on one skinny leg in his corner of the cabin, following along behind through the long days of summer, flying his first uncertain flights over the forests, then as he had been of late, mastering the sky, his broad wings taking him to incredible heights.

He thought of Kise and the farm near Edmonton, of Parsnip, the cow, and tried to remember how the foaming buckets of warm milk had smelled and tasted. He pictured Buck and Blue, the draft horses, and Speck and Melinda, the hounds. He wondered if Kise still played cribbage with Elmore Claridge, and the sound of their voices came back to him, drifting up the stairwell with the stove heat to his bed. "Fifteen two, four, and a pair is six." Kise's triumphal, "Elmore, why don't you learn how to play this game?" All so far away and long ago. Would he ever see a human being again?

By morning the snow was so deep it had drifted to the eaves of the cabin and covered the windows so that no light entered. With such an insulating blanket the cabin was warm and snug, but when David opened the cabin door, he had to tunnel upward to reach the surface. As he peered from his snowy burrow, he saw that the snowfall was continuing unabated. The wind sucked his breath away, and the driving flakes stung his face. Shivering uncontrollably, he backed down the tunnel and into his lair.

Without light from the windows the coal-oil lamp was a godsend. He kept the lamp centered in the middle of the table so as not to risk breaking it. It gave a cheery, fluttering light, strong enough to work by.

Before the storm he had split several canes of spruce and laid them in the rafters to season. Now by the light of the lamp, he made himself a pair of snowshoes by steaming the wood over boiling water from his kettle and warping the spruce into the shape of long, slender teardrops. Once the frames were done, he bound them into place with rawhide; then cut long water-soaked moosehide strips, which he wove into a net across the frame; then knotted a crude harness for each boot.

It was a rough job, but as the moosehide dried in the heat of the cabin, it contracted and hardened into a tough fiber, making the job look almost professional.

When, at last, the storm let up, he stuffed his clothes with skins against the subzero cold and crawled up through the tunnel, dragging his new snowshoes behind him. Unused to the brilliance of the sun on snow after the dim light of the cabin, he sat in the mouth of his burrow, adapting his eyes by stages to the glare.

The cabin and its adjoining piles of firewood were only mounds in the snow, and the stovepipe was a small volcano belching blue smoke from a nether world. In the drifted areas the smaller trees would be completely buried until spring.

He had never used snowshoes before, and his first step in the dry powder was taken with the supremely confident feeling that if he could build a pair of snowshoes he ought to be able to use them. He caught the tail of one under the nose of the other, tripped, fell on his face, rose, tripped, and fell again. On the next try one foot came out of the binding, and he sank up to his hips in soft powder. A gray jay mocked him from a spruce, and David would have thrown a snowball at it had the snow not been too dry to pack. When at last he tried his next step, it was cautiously, and humbly. Little by little he moved forward, leaving

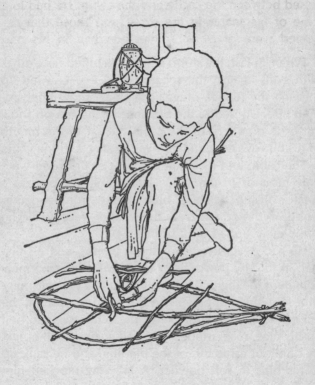

monstrous tracks, stopping now and then to adjust his straps.

Already the wildlife had adapted to the new world. Everywhere were tracks of foxes, hares, squirrels, lynxes, and ptarmigan. A group of five wolves had passed between the cache and the cabin. He had lost some of his snares in the snow, and those that remained were precious, so he kept half in reserve. Now with the snow covering the ground, the hares moved along packed highways and snaring would be easy. He made a few sets, then, exhausted from his snowshoeing, returned to the safety of his burrow.

The next day was clear and colder. His hands quickly numbed through their coating of skins, and his lungs burned with every slow, careful breath. His cheeks felt taut enough to crack. In the surrounding forest he could hear trees exploding with a sound like the report of a musket. So dangerous was the glare on the snow that he covered his eyes and looked at the world through slits. He had been snow-blind once as a child and wanted no part of the dizziness and nausea that followed.

He checked his snares, but of the three hares caught, all had been eaten by foxes in the long hours of darkness. Reading the telltale tracks in the snow, he found where several hares had been killed during the night. The tracks were eloquent: four hares by foxes, two by owls, one by a lynx, and three by wolves. The supply of hares had once seemed limitless; now he hoped it would last the winter.

Near camp he saw tracks where a covey of ptarmigan had passed, leaving small troughs in the snow as they headed for a patch of willow. Much as he hated to hunt the friendly birds, he saw no reason to leave them for the foxes. Taking his bow from its hook near the stove, he strung it, crawled out the tunnel, strapped on his snowshoes, and set out in pursuit.

The tracks ended in the willows, where the covey were busy eating buds. They blended well with the snow, though their dark eyes gave them away.

Drawing an arrow from his quiver, he placed it across his bow, and with numbed fingers prepared to shoot. As he drew it back, the bow snapped and shivered into a dozen pieces. "No!" David cried, hating himself for his ignorance. Of course the bow had broken. The weapon had been warm, and the change of temperature from the cabin to the out-of-doors had been too rapid. The birds gazed at him with calm unconcern as though to say, "We know you wouldn't hurt us." Turning quietly in his tracks, David went back to his hut.

The next morning he was up at daybreak checking his snares, but the predators in the forest had beaten him once more, and one big timber wolf had dragged both hare and snare away. A vague unrest filled him. He climbed to the cache and shoveled the snow away from his supplies to inventory them. Enough tea to last the winter and sufficient stores of dried greens to keep him healthy, but meat was in short supply. Holding to a scant, minimum diet, he could hold out for maybe seventy days. No more.

He wondered what death by starvation would be

like. Well, he would go on as long as the food held out, then he would stop putting wood on the fire. "Cold," Archie had said once, "is the great mercy killer." Until the time came, he would go on living each day as it came.

Soon the snows came again, covering up his trails through the woods. His cabin became only a gentle mound in the drifts; even the stovepipe failed to reach the surface, but left a melt hole blacked by soot from the spruce resins David burned in the fire. Often of a morning David found fresh wolf tracks in the snow, as though they had scented the dried meat hanging from the rafters of the cabin and were considering digging down through the roof.

He avoided going out into the storms. He lay on his bed in darkness to conserve coal oil and listened to sounds. There were times when he thought he heard aircraft, or even voices shouting his name, but he lay still without rushing up the tunnel to listen. He had been fooled so many times now, and the disappointment of making the effort and finding it in vain was worse than not checking at all. The wind in the spruces could sound like a tractor, like a woman sobbing, like anything at all. Stick your head out of the tunnel and the wind would only laugh, and fill your face with snow and your heart with ice.

The snow came without mercy. Driven by the wind off the clearings, it piled about the clumps of trees, then, as the wind changed, eroded away and moved deeper into the forest, as though seeking a final, peaceful resting place. The cache, which had seemed so high and secure when the ground was bare, now lay almost within reach. He dug the dry powder away beneath, fearful that wolverines might raid his supplies, but the wind laughed at him and undid his work.

The next morning he saw tracks in the snow where a squatty animal had trailed through the drifts and paused to sniff at his chimney. His cache wore a fresh mantle of white and looked undisturbed, but the tracks led straight to the tower. Uttering a cry of rage, David climbed up the rungs, knowing even before he peered over the platform what he would see. The great yellow and brown devil of a wolverine had somehow pulled himself over the lip of the platform, devoured his meat, torn open cans of dried greens, and generally so fouled the cache that David's stomach churned at the thought of using what remained.

It was all so unfair! He had been trying so hard to survive, yet all nature seemed to conspire against him. Only enough dried meat left in the cache to cover the palm of his hand. Hanging from the rafters of the cabin was a reserve of enough meat for perhaps two weeks, yet there were months and months of bitter winter before the snow melted. Frightened, he went out into the bitter cold to check his snares. Tracks of foxes, wolves, and lynxes were everywhere, all competing feverishly for the last remaining hares in the forest.

He found fresh tracks where a hare had been gnawing the tender tips of a dwarf birch and had been eaten in turn by a lynx. The hungry cat had eaten bones, hair, and all and even licked up the bloody snow. His snares were empty and there were no more fresh tracks along the runs.

As he ranged farther and farther away from his cabin, he watched for buffaloes and moose. Sometimes his imagination played tricks on him and he thought he saw dark objects in thickets, but each time closer investigation proved him wrong. The game had moved out with the storm, and he could not risk long journeys to find them out. One afternoon he saw a number of large snowy owls. They perched close to the ground and blinked at him with great yellow eyes as he passed, but by morning they had passed on southward, looking for better hunting grounds.

After his unsuccessful forays into the forest, his hot tea became a ritual. He came in leather-mouthed from the dry cold and melted huge quantities of snow to get a few cups of water. Shaving a small plug from a block of tea with his knife, he boiled up a black, bitter concoction and poured it into a cup; then sat on a block of wood near the stove, cup cradled in his hands, absorbing its warmth through his skin while he sipped slowly, letting the hot fluid course down his throat.

The ptarmigan flock were reduced now in number as they fell prey to foxes and lynxes. They stayed tantalizingly close to him, fluttering a few short feet out of reach whenever he moved in their direction. One morning in exasperation he threw a stick at the flock, and they whirled into the air and left for safer thickets, but one of their number lay dead in the snow. Hardly believing his eyes, David sprang at the dead bird like an animal, tripped on his snowshoes, and wallowed in the snow trying to right himself.

He had a wild, desperate feeling something was going to get the bird before he did, but at last he caught it up and carried it back to his lair. He ate the crop with its handful of birch buds first, then roasted and devoured the rest, sucking the bones for their marrow. When he had finished only bones and feathers remained.

Somehow the taste of the food only made him crave more. Three days later he devoured the last of his meat supply. Alarmed, he rose at daylight and tried to find more ptarmigan, but the covey had not returned. All the short northern day he tramped the thickets, finding only a few birch buds to eat.

That night, exhausted, he lay in his bed. He left the lamp burning, needing its company, and as the flame flickered, he watched the shadows it made on the roof. Where was Rusty now? he wondered. Dead, most likely. His plan had seemed so foolproof. Surely if Rusty had made it to civilization, someone would have observed him, captured him, and taken the band off his leg. Somehow, he realized, the plan must have gone sour or by now they would have come to his rescue.

The cabin was hot and uncomfortable; rising from his bed, he opened the door, relishing the cool air flowing in from the tunnel. Faintly from the world outside, he heard strange yelps. Wolves! Hungry wolves, maybe killing each other. Snarls and an excited chorus. Wolves in full cry of the chase. But chasing what? A bison wandering through the land, looking for shoots of willow and birch sticking up through the snow?

As he crept up the tunnel, he heard the distant angry, grunting bellow of an animal in pain. Trembling from excitement, he crouched in the opening of his burrow. Dark shapes moved in the thickets fifty yards away. A huge cow moose had trampled the snow into an arena and was defending herself against a pack of wolves, taking all comers, striking sharp, lethal blows with flailing hooves. Already trampled into the snow was one wolf, perhaps a youngster, who had dared too much.

The wolves were patient, knowing that time was on their side, for the cow was winter-weak and tiring fast.

Again and again David crept back to his stove for warmth. Time dragged on. Would the fight never end? A huge black male wolf, who had been sitting on his haunches watching, suddenly rose to his feet and walked stiffly in a full circle about the moose, as though testing her condition. Then, more swiftly, he cried again as another wolf made a short, distracting rush at her nose. In a flash the black wolf took advantage of the ruse, slashing the hamstring muscles of a back leg. Valiantly the moose tried to stay upright, but her hindquarters buckled and suddenly she was down and aswarm with snarling, yelping wolves.

David was not to be denied a share. Grasping his axe, he darted from his tunnel and rushed straight at the startled wolves. He could see their great yellow eyes, the thick ruff about their necks, and hackles of stiff hair rising from their backs. The great black male, snarling a bloody-jawed challenge, made a short rush at the intruder to frighten him away, but David shouted his own challenge, however nervous, and advanced. He could almost taste the meat. Aiming at the challenger, he hurled his axe with all his remaining strength. It struck the wolf on the rib cage and bounced off harmlessly, but the animal yelped in surprise, and slowly the pack thought it best to yield. One by one they retreated to the thickets, where they lay panting, sending up moist clouds of breath from their exertions, waiting for the intruder to go away.

Taking up his axe, David cut open the jugular, letting the hot blood gush into the snow. He worked quickly, warming his hands from time to time on the hot flesh while he cut out quarter by quarter with the axe and chopped the meat into pieces small enough to handle. By the time he had carried the last of the meat to his tunnel, it was already glazed with ice. For a long moment, he stood over the carcass, glaring at the wolves. He managed a great growl of dominion, then, giggling foolishly, sprinted for his tunnel, leaving the plundered remains to their rightful owners. Moments later he heard the cracking of bones, and when he peered out, the carcass was once more aswarm with wolves.

Seventeen

WITH the threat of starvation averted, David hoped to settle in for a safe, uneventful winter, snug in his burrow, but he failed to reckon with another scourge of the north—cabin fever.

It began innocuously enough with increasing tensions, an irritability foreign to his general complacent nature. Bumping his head one day on his doorway, he burst into sudden violence, beating the offending log with his fists, an ordeal that left him frightened and exhausted. "I won't do that again," he vowed, "or I'll never make it through the winter." But a week later he dropped a piece of stove wood on his foot and flew into a blinding rage.

Soon his imagination began to play wild tricks on him. Once as he crawled from his burrow into the light, he saw Kise coming toward him in the snow. Kise was smiling, holding out his arms to him. David ran forward shouting, only to stumble in the soft drifts without his snowshoes, and when he righted himself, the illusion had faded. He became frightened of losing his sanity, fearing that he could not long keep himself under control.

It was best, he decided, when he kept busy, so when he could not go outdoors, he carved wooden animals in the dim light of his lamp. In all but the fiercest weather he forced himself to go out for exercise, hunting, though he no longer needed the food. He made Xs on the wall to keep track of the days, and as the marks grew in number so did his spirits, for he knew that with many marks on the wall spring could not be long in coming.

And then one morning as he crawled from his entrance he felt a warm wind blowing from the south, and the snow packed so well he made himself a snowman with a stick for a nose, and felt the better for its company. Soon his roof showed bare, and the bottom of his tunnel became a puddle of melted snow. Whatever spring storms might still be in the offing, winter was behind him.

The gentle ptarmigan that survived the long winter had already traded their snowy winter plumage for the blending browns of summer and migrated farther north to their nesting grounds on the barrens when David got ready to break camp. He had stayed longer than he planned because spring had been a happy time of new arrivals. One day the black spruces had been silent, save for laughing jays and clonking ravens; the next, every thicket seemed bursting with birds. Besides, the meadow, gay now with emergent wildflowers, had come to be home to him.

But he knew he had to leave. He told himself that Kise needed him on the farm, though, way down deep, he had grown to know it was he who needed Kise. Not forever, but for a time yet. And although Archie never talked about kinsfolk, there had to be someone out there who deserved to know what happened to the pilot.

David cured what meat he could carry on the trail, gathered his snares, and built a scabbard of moose-hide for his axe. Leaving a supply of food sealed in tins for anyone who might come along in need, he latched the door against entry by animals, then set off across the meadow bound for the river.

The day was sunny and warm. The ice had vanished from the ponds, and everywhere mallard drakes in fierce attendance upon their chosen hens were making nuptial pursuits high in the air. Geese honked, squealed, or yelped, depending upon their species, as they passed high overhead, eager for arctic wetlands farther north. Three-toed woodpeckers and flickers drummed from sounding boards high in the trees. A thousand birds voiced their territorial hymns in mass chorus, each staking out his own little piece of the seemingly limitless north.

At the far edge of the meadow David paused, say-

ng good-bye to the sights, sounds, scents, and moods
that had been his life for half a year. Some day when
he was older, perhaps, he would come back here to
live. "When I'm older?" he thought. "I am older!" He
had had a birthday back there in winter when things
were bleakest, and even had he known the date, it
would probably have gone unnoticed in the press of
daily emergencies. He was fourteen and a half now,
which is almost fifteen. And to David, fifteen—well
that was almost sixteen, an age when he would become a young man rather than a boy.

He could have sat there all day, but the thought of
the journey ahead brought him back to reality. He
stood up, shouldered his pack, and set out for the
river. Once there he would have to figure out where
his best chance lay, whether to follow the river
upstream or downstream to reach civilization.

Suddenly, just as he was about to leave the glade,
he heard a vaguely familiar sound, a bugling high in
the heavens. "Kerloo! Kerloo! Kerloo!" His eyes
watered from the brightness of the sunny skies and
he sneezed violently. There! He saw them! Two
bright, gleaming stars, two great white whooping
cranes shouting down their joy upon the land.

"Rusty!" David shouted, abandoning his gear and
sprinting out of the trees that had almost swallowed
him.

The birds seemed to ignore him, floating easily in
the upper air with only an occasional slow beat of the
wings to maintain elevation. Slowly the circles wid-

ened, and almost imperceptibly, the cranes began their long glide toward earth.

David held his breath. At this point their course could easily have altered and taken them to other clearings miles away. He watched them descend, trying hard to pick out which one was his friend, but both looked the same.

"Rusty!" he shouted again.

"Kerloo! Kerleoo!" One of the cranes answered as though in greeting, but just as he was sure it was Rusty, the other crane bugled too.

Then, as the birds swept over the meadow, they split up, one landing at some distance across the meadow while the other glided on toward David. "Kerloo! Kerloo!" he called as he sailed in and came to a bouncing halt almost at David's feet.

Tears of joy spurted down David's cheeks. He threw his arms about his friend. "Aark!" Rusty complained, unused to such an embrace. Standing at full height, the other whooping crane paced back and forth nervously, trying to decide whether to stay or flee. It trumpeted loud, angry warnings, as though i found the whole scene one of certain disaster.

David stood back and regarded Rusty with awe The band he had placed on his leg was gone, who knew where. The rusty feathers had been supplante by the wondrous snowy splendor of the adult. Eve his eyes had changed from soft, trusting brown t fierce, authoritarian yellow. Already the skin of th forehead was losing its tiny feathers and turning to pale rose color. David spoke softly to the bird, an

he bird answered, no longer in a querulous and uncertain voice, but with a fine throaty new bass.

But somewhere inside that dignified figure the
merry, fun-loving Rusty of old had to remain. David
picked up a stick and tossed it into the air, and Rusty
whooped instantly with delight, spread his great wings
as though herding a snake, seized the stick in his beak,
and with a short flapping hop, skip, and jump, tossed
it high again. Suddenly David was flapping his arms,
leaping, spinning wildly and recklessly with Rusty,
caught up in the age-old dance, outdoing the crane at
every turn.

Out in the meadow the wild crane flapped his
wings and gave a short hop, as though wanting to join
but a bit nervous and uncertain.

When, helpless with laughter, puffing and chuffing,
David staggered to the sidelines to catch his breath,
Rusty composed himself with a shuffling and shaking
of disordered feathers, assumed his former dignity,
and moved off nonchalantly to feed with the other
crane.

A momentary twinge of jealousy crept through
David, but he struggled to put it down. He stood
watching the two birds as they wandered side by side
through the meadow. Rusty's companion found a
tidbit in the vegetation and gave some low, intimate
call, which David could not hear but which called
Rusty over to share. Together they probed the ground,
heads almost touching. The very sight of them increased the boy's loneliness.

A soft, balmy wind floated across the meadow, and

as if by some mysterious signal, Rusty and his friend raised their great wings and lifted into the air. For a long time David watched as their circles took them higher and higher and farther and farther over the vast, lonely forests and muskegs of the north.

David imagined that Archie stood by his side. "A good job, kid. You've finished what we first set out to do, put Rusty back into the wild."

He shouldered his pack. Far off through the trees he could see the shine of the river beckoning him. He moved off without a backward glance at the scenes he had come to love. Someday, when he was of age, perhaps he would return, and maybe Rusty would still remember his human friend and take a few moments off from family duties to dance a wild whooping crane fandango to tunes of lonely winds strumming the lutes of the north.

Eighteen

_____

THE pilot of the observation plane and Bill Sterling, the Audubon Society biologist, huddled out of the prairie wind on the front porch of the Dakota farm. From Aransas Refuge they had flown north by light plane, attempting to follow a family of whooping cranes, but had lost them in cloud cover in the vicinity of Turnbridge Wells. Now while waiting for the weather to clear before proceeding to Canada and Wood Buffalo Park in a study of migration routes, they were investigating reported sightings to add some body to the scant information existing about the rare birds.

Garratt, the local warden, had dismissed McFeeters's report of the autumn before as being one of the myriad false sightings that plague researchers. But to the biologist any lead seemed worth investigating. During migration losses to the tiny population of whoopers were heavy, and it was vital to establish protective measures around all known feeding and resting areas.

"Like I told Garratt last fall," McFeeters told the two men, "that whooping crane was right here in my barnyard. My kid came running into the house, hollering a big bird was after him, but shucks, he just wanted some food. He followed me to the barn and ate some wheat I throwed out for him. Figured he was somebody's pet."

"What happened to him?" the pilot asked.

"Last we saw, the bird was working the dung heap below the barn for night crawlers. By the time the warden got here, of course, he was gone, and folks figured we made the whole story up."

The biologist nodded. "We get lots of false sightings," he explained, "but I'm glad you turned yours in. It might interest you to know you've done a good job describing an immature whooping crane. Normally we would discredit such an unusually late sighting, but a few days after your report, a young bird and a mature bird did arrive at Aransas. My guess would be that your bird took up with another late bird reported along the Platte. What does puzzle me, though, is that you claim the bird was tame."

The farmer nodded vigorously. "Sure he was tame. I didn't tell Garratt—folks would have hoorahed me

ıt of the state—but he was so tame I touched him.
ad a tin band on his leg with some sort of writing
ı it, and I took it off."

"Come on now," Sterling cut in in disbelief.

McFeeters's thin face darkened. "Hell, I can show
ou!" he snapped, jumping from his seat. "I throwed
on a shelf in the old horse barn. I'll be back."

"Looks like it's going to be another one of those
ays," the biologist said to the pilot. "His description
f a young crane is right out of the book. He's a good
bserver, but this crazy stuff—Wow! A tame whoop-
ıg crane with a tin band around his leg with writing
ı it. None of the wild whoopers have ever been
anded, and the captive ones are all accounted for.
low would all this look in my report? You watch. He
on't be able to locate that band."

"Way folks doubt me," McFeeters complained as
e strode up the hill, "you'd think I'd spotted a flying
aucer or something." He held out a piece of rusty
n. "Here! It was attached to the bird's leg, I swear."

The biologist held it up to the light but seemed
nimpressed. "What do you make of it?" he asked,
anding it to the pilot.

For a moment the man regarded the object suspi-
iously. "Hey!" he said suddenly. "This might be a
egitimate SOS! And these figures 'Gr. 143.' That's
ot to be an aircraft identification number. Grumman
43." Carefully he rubbed the tin with his finger tips,
racing the lines and figures. "Here's the latitude and
ongitude of the disabled aircraft, and a name and

address in Edmonton, Alberta. Probably someone to notify."

He shook hands with McFeeters. "If you don' mind, we'll take this along and scramble for the airport. The civil air patrol can check the info and determine whether or not the plane has ever been reported missing."

As they drove out the gate the biologist waved from the rented automobile. "Thanks again, McFeeters You're a good observer. Any time you see a whooping crane or even a flying saucer, let me know. I'l take your word."

That night Sterling had already gone to bed when the pilot knocked on the door of his motel room Blinking in the sudden light, he propped himself on one elbow. "What luck?" he asked.

"The plane's already been found. Last week, just after the snow melt. Some copter pilot making a mineral survey just outside the Wood Buffalo National Park boundaries, happened on the wreckage. Turned out to be a Bureau of Sports Fisheries and Wildlife plane missing since last May on a flight from Edmonton to Yellowknife by way of Fort Smith. Most likely it went down in a late spring storm. The pilot was alone and apparently lived for some time after the crash; he'd made a shelter out of the wreckage. At first when they found the body covered with moss and logs, it looked as though he'd been buried by someone, but they've decided now the debris could havs been deposited by high water on the neighboring pond."

"What about the name on the tag? The guy in Alberta. You check that out?"

The pilot nodded. "I phoned the newspaper in Edmonton, Bill. The guy has a farm a few miles from town. Been a bargeman on northern rivers, trapper, prospector, guide. You name it. Interesting guy. Married a widow with one boy. Couple of years back she died, and last May the boy ran away from home. He was seen at the airport the same day Grumman 143 stopped in Edmonton for servicing. Could be he was a stowaway on that plane."

The biologist whistled under his breath. "Did you ask the air rescue people about that?"

His companion nodded. "They shrugged it off. The copter pilot searched the area and was satisfied that no one else was around. They maintain that even if a boy had survived the crash, most probably he would have died of exposure when winter came. I tried to interest them in a further search, but they turned me down cold. They've no reason to consider the case other than closed."

"Damn!" Sterling complained. "We're no closer than before to finding out how the whooping crane fitted in. My guess would be that some cranes were nesting in the vicinity of the crash, maybe a way-out theory but worth investigating if we were heading into that area. If that boy were still alive, he might tell us things about whoopers we haven't yet considered. The area is well out of their known range, but then, with the whoopers, every year you learn something new."

For a few moments the pilot sat deep in thought, then he cleared his throat. "You know, Bill," he said, "you and I aren't going to sleep very well until we solve this mystery. We're due in Edmonton to have floats put on the plane, and maybe we can learn something from the boy's father."

The biologist looked thoughtful. "Our job was to make a study of whooping crane migration routes from Texas to the Territories, not hunt for a missing kid. But come to think of it, the whooping cranes are tied up in this somehow, and if we stretched a point, hunting for that boy might damn well qualify."

Grinning, the pilot headed toward the door. "See you in the morning," he said. "I'm getting out of here before you change your mind."

Kise was just coming from the barn with a heavy bucket of milk when the two men drove up to the farmhouse. He regarded them with the suspicion most country people have of strangers, and merely stood quietly eyeing them, waiting for them to state their business so he could get on with his. The rented car had Canadian plates, and until they spoke there was nothing to identify the men as Americans. When Sterling spoke Kise's name, however, in the soft accents of the south, he looked at them with new interest.

"Sorry to bother you when you're obviously busy," Sterling said. "We're from the U.S. Fish and Wildlife Service, and we're doing a study of whooping crane migration routes."

Kise changed hands on the bucket rather than set

it down. "Don't reckon I can help you," he said. "I've never even seen a whooping crane."

"We didn't come about that, exactly," Sterling said, "but about your missing son."

Kise almost dropped the pail of milk. "What? David? You know where my boy is?"

"Take it easy, please," the biologist said. "We don't know where your boy is and don't want to raise any false hopes that he's alive and well. But we have reason to believe your boy stowed away in one of our planes, which later crashed up in the Territories. Apparently the pilot or the boy survived long enough to raise a young whooping crane. When the bird migrated south in the fall, he carried a leg band with an SOS and your name and address on it. The plane has been discovered and the pilot's body found, but as yet there has been no sign of a boy. Frankly, only a miracle could have brought him through the winter."

Kise slumped to the porch and sat rubbing his face with his rough hands. "My God," he said. "He was a fine boy, that David. I guess I never stopped hoping I'd look down the lane some day and see him coming home."

"We didn't come here to tell you that he'll never come home," Sterling said. "We're on our way up there in the course of our study of the whooping cranes, and we needed to know anything you might tell us of the boy—how old he was, how he was dressed when you last saw him."

"You'll fly to the crash site?" Kise said eagerly.

"Take me along! Please, take me along. I was raised in the north. Perhaps I'd be of help."

The biologist grinned. "One of the other reasons we came by is we hoped you'd want to come along." He glanced about him. "You can get someone to watch the farm for you?"

Kise nodded.

"We leave tomorrow morning then. We'll drop by for you about daybreak."

The two men watched as Kise picked up his bucket and strode toward the house. "I hope we're doing the right thing," the pilot said. "Anyway, from the looks of him he hasn't gone off whistling like that in years."

David stood on the bank of the river, looking across at the blaze he had made the autumn before, the last of a long series of bright scars leading back over aspen parklands, ponds, and thickets to the wrecked plane. The river was still in spring flood, overflowing its banks and making lakes and backwaters on the low-lying lands. He shuddered to think that he and Rusty had dared cross it even when it was low.

Even though he had some months to plan his departure, he was still undecided as to which direction to travel. Upstream there was a chance of finding miners' camps, or perhaps villages. Downstream, since the maps showed that many of the rivers ended on the shores of Great Slave Lake, he could hope to chance on a family of Indians fishing, or even to signal the great barges freighting supplies to points along the northern shore. Somehow it made more sense to head downstream, so he headed north along the shore.

Taking his axe, he girdled a large aspen tree along the bank with a shining new blaze. Then in the soft, green bark, he carved his name, the month he guessed it was, the year, and the direction of his travel. As he carved he noted that it was more than a year since he had run away.

As he shouldered his pack, he thought back on that year—of Archie hiding his pain in laughter, of Rusty's first awkward steps, of the desperate cold of winter, of the fight with the wolves over the carcass of the moose, and of the greatest thrill of all, Rusty soaring wild and free above the land.

He had hoped to find a trail along the river, but if any traveled his way, they avoided the jackstraws of fallen timber and went by water. David had little choice but to work his way through the thickets, confident, somehow, that whatever the difficulty, every step brought him that much closer to civilization.

Sometimes he sought easier passage away from the river on higher ground; sometimes he was forced to follow the banks of tributaries until he found logs on which to cross, but no matter how far he wandered from the great brown stream, its whereabouts was always firmly in mind. Whenever he returned to the river after an absence, he had a feeling that he had just missed something, that a boat had just floated past.

How delicious his diet was now compared to the winter months'. There were fresh duck eggs to be had daily as well as quantities of greens for salads. Sometimes when he found a new nest, he paused to rest, built a fire, and made an omelette on the spot.

Life was better now; he felt somehow in control, able to cope with any situation that might arise. "I don't know where I am," he muttered to himself one day, "but at least I'm not lost."

It was Kise's first plane ride, and he was in a talkative mood as the plane droned northward. "See that river down there," he said. "She don't look so mighty from up here, but I've seen those innocent-looking rapids swallow a barge, cargo and all. Years back I helped man a barge of gasoline down her, bound for Yellowknife. We were all summer getting there. And there on that bend I camped when I was a boy with my folks, and we made our living selling fresh meat and fish to the boat crews as they came by. Those days men trapped or freighted; nowdays everyone's hunting for minerals and oil."

The first night they spent in Fort Smith, and the next day they were airborne again, searching until at last they sighted the wreckage of the plane on the shore of the pond. The pond was barely large enough to set the plane down in, but down they went and both men grinned when they looked back on landing and saw Kise still covering his eyes.

For a few minutes they wandered about the deserted camp in silence. Kise scraped his toe in the ashes of the campfire. "Last year's ashes," he said. For a time the old woodsman disappeared in the forest, then suddenly he was back. "Someone left here running a blaze line due north, straight enough to follow from the air. I pray it was my boy."

They returned to the plane and took off. At times as they flew they lost the blaze line from the air and circled, skimming the trees, until they located it again. They landed on a lake and found David's camp on a point jutting out into the water. "Showed good sense, whoever it was," Kise remarked. "Camped on this spit of land to escape the insects."

Kise rode up front with the pilot now, holding the thin map like a magic talisman in his hands, watching for the landmarks that David had indicated. First the broad river heading north, then the knoll lording it over the flat monotony of the lands and the cabin. Their spirits soared when they spotted the cabin and fell when they flew time and again just over the rooftop and found it deserted. It was only when they landed and found an aspen tree along the river bearing David's freshly carved name and date that they knew that somewhere, two weeks or so ahead of them down that raging river, the boy they were seeking was miraculously still alive.

To David the roar of the aircraft was only faintly audible above the sound of the river. He whirled in his tracks, listened, then dropped his pack from his shoulders. A single-engined aircraft with unwieldy landing floats was flying downstream, barely skim-

ming the trees. Dashing into the shallows, David
waved his arms, splashed water with his hands, and
shouted.

For long agonizing moments as the plane passed
downstream, he thought he had not been seen. Then
suddenly, he saw the plane bank, and soon it was
flying back upstream.

Holding his arms high, he pointed to a bend
quarter of a mile downstream where the flooding
river had spilled over its banks to make a quiet backwater, large enough for a plane to use for landing.
Then, unimpeded by his pack, he rushed along the
edge of the stream signaling, imploring the plane to
follow.

As David waited impatiently along the shore, the
pilot made run after run at the river, inspecting the
surface for hidden obstacles. Each time the plane
lifted once more into the air, David felt that he was
being deserted. "Perhaps," he thought, "with my
wild hair I look like a savage and they think I'm
dangerous."

At last, however, the plane touched down, splashed
along the surface, then settled deeper as the pilot cut
the power and taxied toward shore. Suddenly David
was overcome with shyness, with an impulse to flee
to run and hide like an animal until the strangers had
gone.

But before he could act, the engine ceased, the
pontoons glided shoreward, and he was suddenly
knee-deep in water, holding the floats steady against
the tug of the current, yet keeping them from bang

ng on rocks. He knew the men were staring down at him, and he was glad to be busy so that he did not have to look at their faces.

"David! How are you, boy?" Kise, fit but grayer, crawled down off one wing and stepped along a float, holding the struts for balance. In seconds they were laughing and pounding each other.

"I found a cabin, Kise, and made it through the winter all alone," David explained. "It's a great place; I wish you could see it." He paused as a thought occurred to him. "How on earth did you find me?"

Kise grinned. "I'll let Mr. Sterling here explain."

Sterling held up the metal leg band. "From the look in David's face he's seen this band before."

David took the band from him and looked it over. "That's the band all right. I never thought I'd see it again."

The men set up camp on a knoll above the river, and sitting before a campfire, David told them, the words coming out in a rush, of Archie, of the plane crash, of the band on Rusty's leg, of the long trek and brutal winter at the cabin.

Kise watched the boy with pride and wonder shining on his face. "I've been running the old place alone, David," he said. "It sure will be good having you home again."

As the plane skipped across the water and labored into the air, David's stomach tightened with an unexpected memory of Archie's crash, but soon he relaxed and watched curiously as the country unfolded before him.

"Look down there, David," the pilot said. "
highway bridging the river. Looks like in about tw
more weeks you'd have made it out on your own."

They passed over the vast icebound waters of Grea
Slave Lake, a body so huge David imagined it to b
an ocean. Near Yellowknife they landed, and Davi
and Kise bid good-bye to the biologist and the pilo
and boarded a commercial plane for Edmonton.

David hugged the window, staring down at north
ern scenes he had known and loved for more than
year of his life. Trails left by herds of wood buffal
crisscrossed the land. Two big white birds flew nor
on the horizon. Probably they were swans, but mayb
it would be all right if he imagined they were whoo
ing cranes. He tried to fight back the moistu
gathering in his eyes.

Kise touched his shoulder. "Don't be ashamed
loving the north, David. There's a spell about her th
gets in the marrow of a man's bones and won't soa
away with a hot bath. Home, though, we've got
farm needs tending and a couple of old hound do
will be right glad to see you. I guess it would plea
your ma too if you got a mite more formal schoolin
Then, someday, maybe we can head back nor
together."

David grinned. Already he could hear Speck ar
Melinda baying, hear the old work team nickeri
across the morning pastures for their grain, ar
Parsnip, the milk cow, groaning, udder tight with t
morning's milk and needing him desperately.

NON-FICTION

☐ ARTHUR FORD SPEAKS FROM BEYOND—Sullivan	Q2866	1.50
☐ BED/TIME/STORY—Robinson	X2540	1.75
☐ BIG JULIE OF VEGAS—Linn	X2564	1.75
☐ EIGHT IS ENOUGH—Braden	23002-3	1.75
☐ FELTON & FOWLER'S BEST, WORST & MOST UNUSUAL—Felton & Fowler	23020-1	1.95
☐ THE GIRLS OF NEVADA—Vigliotti	C2595	1.95
☐ HOLLYWOOD TRAGEDY—Carr	22889-4	1.95
☐ HOW TO MAKE YOUR MAN MORE SENSITIVE—D. & D. O'Connor	22961-0	1.95
☐ THE INTRUDERS—Montandon	22963-7	1.95
☐ PRIMAL SENSUALITY—Newhorn	X2394	1.75
☐ THE WOMAN SAID YES—West	23128-3	1.95
☐ ANN LANDERS SPEAKS OUT	Q3305	1.50
☐ IT'S ALL IN THE STARS—Zolar	X3566	1.75
☐ JENNIFER'S BOYS—Sills	X3519	1.75
☐ MOON MADNESS—Abel	13697-3	1.75
☐ PEAK SEX—Drs. Feldman & Feldman	13637-X	1.75
☐ THE PSYCHIC POWER OF ANIMALS—Schul	13724-4	1.75
☐ THE SECRET POWER OF PYRAMIDS—Schul & Pettit	X3273	1.75
☐ FROM PLATO TO NIETZCHE—Allen *(Former title. Guide Book to Western Thought)	Q768	1.50
☐ THE PSYCHIC POWER OF PYRAMIDS—Schul & Pettit	90001-0	3.95

Buy them at your local bookstores or use this handy coupon for ordering:

FAWCETT PUBLICATIONS, P.O. Box 1014, Greenwich Conn. 06830

Please send me the books I have checked above. Orders for less than 5 books must include 60c for the first book and 25c for each additional book to cover mailing and handling. Orders of 5 or more books postage is Free. I enclose $_____ in check or money order.

Mr/Mrs/Miss_____

Address_____

City_____ State/Zip_____

Please allow 4 to 5 weeks for delivery. This offer expires 6/78.

A-15